"You found a body?"

Ruth gave him a don't-you-dare-mess-with-me look.

"I did," Eric said.

"Is it my husband?"

"No, the remains are female."

Ruth seemed to deflate, but only for a moment. Then she walked into the shed. Eric followed.

Two deputies were moving boxes away from the corpse. It was crowded, hot and dark in the building. One of the cops put down the basket he'd just picked up. It teetered on the edge and fell to the ground with a thump.

At that moment, more than anything, Eric wished he'd stayed outside, because when the basket fell over, Eric spotted another dead body.

Books by Pamela Tracy

Love Inspired Suspense

Pursuit of Justice #46
The Price of Redemption #77

PAMELA TRACY

lives in Arizona with a newly acquired husband *(Yes, Pamela is somewhat a newlywed. You can be a newlywed for seven years. We're only on year five.)* and a confused cat *(Hey, I had her all to myself for fifteen years. Where'd this guy come from? But, maybe it's okay. He's pretty good about feeding me and petting me.)* and a toddler *(Newlymom is almost as fun as newlywed!)*. She was raised in Omaha, Nebraska, and started writing at age twelve *(A very bad teen romance featuring David Cassidy from* The Partridge Family*)*. Later, she honed her writing skills while earning a B.A. in Journalism at Texas Tech University in Lubbock, Texas *(And wrote a very bad science fiction novel that didn't feature David Cassidy.)*.

Readers can write to her at www.pamelakayetracy.com, or c/o Steeple Hill Books, 233 Broadway, Suite 1001, New York, NY 10279.

The Price of Redemption
PAMELA TRACY

Steeple
Hill®

Published by Steeple Hill Books™

STEEPLE HILL BOOKS

Steeple
Hill®

ISBN-13: 978-0-373-44267-6
ISBN-10:   0-373-44267-X

THE PRICE OF REDEMPTION

Copyright © 2007 by Pamela Tracy Osback

All rights reserved. Except for use in any review, the reproduction or utilization of this work in whole or in part in any form by any electronic, mechanical or other means, now known or hereafter invented, including xerography, photocopying and recording, or in any information storage or retrieval system, is forbidden without the written permission of the editorial office, Steeple Hill Books, 233 Broadway, New York, NY 10279 U.S.A.

This is a work of fiction. Names, characters, places and incidents are either the product of the author's imagination or are used fictitiously, and any resemblance to actual persons, living or dead, business establishments, events or locales is entirely coincidental.

This edition published by arrangement with Steeple Hill Books.

® and TM are trademarks of Steeple Hill Books, used under license. Trademarks indicated with ® are registered in the United States Patent and Trademark Office, the Canadian Trade Marks Office and in other countries.

www.SteepleHill.com

Printed in U.S.A.

Let love and faithfulness never leave you; bind them around your neck, write them on the tablet of your heart. Then you will win favor and a good name in the sight of God and man.

—*Proverbs* 3:3–4

They say it takes a village to raise a child. In my case a village helped me realize my dreams of publication, and there are many, many villagers who need special thanks.

First, to the members of the Loaded Pencils critique group (established 1993 and still going) who taught me most of what I know: Betty Hufford, Stacy Cornell, Karen Lenzen, Dana McNeely, Bill Haynes and Mark Henley.

Next, to the members of the CCLP critique group (established 2002 and still going) who keep me on task and tell me when I'm meandering: Cathy McDavid, Libby Banks and Connie Flynn.

Also, to my last-minute readers, who catch my silly mistakes: Stacy Cornell, Elizabeth Weed, and Stacey Rannik.

Last, to the editors who make it all come together: Jessica Alvarez, Krista Stroever and Becky Germany.

The word *thanks* doesn't seem to say enough.

ONE

It wasn't his first dead body. Or even his second.

In truth, if Eric Santellis needed to, he could, off the top of his head, remember standing over roughly four, no five, corpses. All died violently. One had been his best friend. Two had been relatives. Two had been strangers who'd had the bad luck and bad judgment to mess with one of his brothers.

But this dead body scared him more than all the others—even though there was no way he could be fingered for her death.

Nope, Eric figured this woman had been dead awhile and he had an airtight alibi courtesy of Florence Prison. And her discovery guaranteed him a spot on the front page of every major newspaper—again.

Unable to stand the stench any longer, Eric stumbled across the shed's uneven flooring. In places, the boards had given in to age, neglect, and some spots were little more than earth. He tripped up the two narrow steps leading outside and to fresh air, sunlight and wide-open spaces. A moment later, he thought there might not be enough fresh air in the world to rid his nostrils of the stench of his discovery. Once he could breathe again, he flipped open his cell phone and started searching for a location that might allow a signal. Reception, here in the middle of nowhere, was hit-and-miss.

He found a spot and soon connected with the local authorities and a dispatcher. "Sheriff's Office. How can I help you?" She sounded all of twelve years old.

"Yes, I'm at 723 Prospector's Way. I've just discovered a body in my shed."

"Are you sure the person is deceased?"

"Very sure."

"Your name please?"

"Eric Santellis."

His family had helped establish this small town more than a hundred years ago. His last name often rendered the good people of Broken Bones speechless. Otherwise, he'd have mistaken the silence for a lost connection.

The dispatcher finally cleared her throat. "Did you say Santellis?"

"Yes, I'm at my cabin. There's a body in my shed. It's been there awhile. It's in pretty bad shape and—"

"I'll get a deputy out there immediately."

The silence returned, but this time he could legitimately blame a lost connection. He returned the phone to his pocket, and with nothing else to do but wait, stared at the cabin that had been in his family forever.

Family. That word should conjure up good memories and a lifetime of nurturing. It didn't. But, then, good memories and nurturing were not the stuff the Santellis clan was known for. His grandfather, who'd left him the land and falling-down buildings, had been a bitter old man. Eric had been more than surprised twenty years ago when he'd inherited this place.

It was Eric's last piece of the Santellis fortune.

When he'd entered Florence Prison, his net worth probably figured in the millions if you considered his family's fortune. When he'd left prison just three months ago, he no longer had family; they no longer had a fortune. His two older brothers were dead, his father had advanced Alzheimer's and his sister and younger brother had disappeared. Without anyone standing guard, the misbegotten gains of the Santellis crime family fell victim to his sisters-in-law's lawyers and to the government. Eric would have turned it all over without an argument.

The empire was a legacy paid for with blood—starting with that of his ancestor who'd built this cabin more than a hundred years ago. This land, this cabin, was one of the few Santellis holdings the government hadn't claimed.

Of course, that all might change now that a deceased female had taken up residence in his shed.

Sirens echoed in the distance and a cloud of dust appeared. Eric headed for his porch and sat to await chaos and suspicion. Three vehicles arrived. First came the sheriff's SUV. It quickly bumped over the dirt driveway that led to Eric's porch and skidded to a stop. A few minutes later, and taking the bumps at a precarious speed, a sedan bearing the same logo pulled in behind the sheriff. The deputies parked near the cabin and jumped out—the dispatcher probably hadn't understood what Eric meant when he said the body had been in his shed 'awhile.' Hurrying was unnecessary. Then, surprise, surprise, came a third vehicle, a Cadillac not from the sheriff's department. It carefully moved up the driveway, parked close to the porch, and a tall, white-haired man climbed out.

The deputies stayed huddled by the sheriff, but the older man came on the porch and said, "James Winters. Call me 'Doc', everyone does. I'm the local doctor, retired, but in a pinch, I'm all they have. I hear you've found a dead body."

So the twelve-year-old had gotten something right. "Very dead."

"I believe you, son."

The sheriff slammed the door of his SUV. The noise echoed in the silence of the forsaken land Eric now called home. The deputies followed as the sheriff ambled toward Eric. The sheriff, older, chubby, dark-haired and balding didn't bother to introduce himself or show a badge. He snarled, "Did you touch anything?"

"Yes," Eric admitted. "I thought I had a dead animal in there. While I was looking for it, I moved some boxes and stacks of junk. I was tossing old clothes into a laundry basket when I accidentally took hold of the arm. Of course, I didn't know it was an arm at first. That's when whatever was covering her dislodged, and I saw a skull and realized what I was holding."

"You might want to call a lawyer," the doctor advised. "Before you say anything else."

"No need," he said wryly. "There's no way they can pin this on me. I'm guessing she took her last breath at least six months ago, and back then I was a guest of the Arizona penal system."

"No kidding," said the doctor, clearly surprised.

"Your second day here and you've already got trouble." The sheriff stared at Eric before slowly taking a small notebook out of his shirt pocket and writing down a few things. Then, he added, "Well, let's take a look."

"I smelled decay yesterday." Eric headed for the shed. "At first, I figured a cat or something."

He'd been wrong. Dead wrong.

"This morning, I couldn't take the smell anymore."

That the shed was in one piece was nothing short of astounding. It had actually been built before the main cabin, and Eric's ancestors had lived in it while they finished building their permanent residence. The sheriff opened the door and started to take a tentative step. The putrid odor caused him to pause, and then he took a rubber glove from his pocket, held it to his nose and entered. Boards creaked in protest. They creaked even louder after the two deputies, sans the rubber gloves, joined their boss. Eric and the doctor waited a moment.

"I thought I read you got out of jail almost six months ago?" Doc said.

"No, that's when the paperwork started. It took about three months to get it through the system."

"System's a joke," Doc said, and headed for the shed.

Eric's lantern still hung from a nail. Its glow, inadequate for the task, simply made the room look spooky. Eric lit a second lantern, and both deputies pulled out flashlights. One immediately started gagging and headed for the door. The doctor applied vapor rub under his nose and handed the jar to Eric. Then, he took out his flashlight and moved toward the far wall and the body. Bending down, he made a careful perusal of the area. Taking out a minirecorder, he said, "First assessment. Remains appear to be of a woman between the age of thirty and fifty. She's been discovered in a shed and exposed to carnivores."

The sheriff moved closer and started taking pictures. He glanced at Eric. "What made you think she'd been dead about six months?"

"I have a degree in criminal justice. Finished it while in prison. Plus, I've seen dead bodies."

"Not a bad guess, but you forgot to allow for the heat." Winters returned to his recorder. "Based on the level of deterioration, the female has already started..."

Eric left the room. He didn't need to hear any more. While the body was badly decomposed, it didn't take a scientist to judge it female, since it was wearing a faded pink polyester pantsuit. Still, Eric would have blown his assessment of the corpse's age, putting her in her seventies or thereabouts based on the style of clothes.

He headed back to his front porch and sat, waiting. Doc Winters was soon replaced by the coroner. Soon, another law enforcement officer arrived. This one had a bigger camera. The man didn't meet Eric's eyes and didn't bother to introduce himself.

But then, the sheriff hadn't offered a name, either.

But Eric knew who he was. Rich Mallery. His family had settled the area, alongside Eric's family. Rich's family stayed in the area and went into law enforcement, politics and land speculation. Eric's family left for the city and kept law enforcement busy, paid off politicians and watched as blood soaked the land.

Eric's family demanded attention; Eric wanted none of it. He'd been at the cabin two days without a single visitor, a dream come true.

Trust his family to ruin everything.

He wondered which brother, or brother-in-law, was responsible for the Jane Doe in the shed.

* * *

"This is the sixth cop in ten years. It's a cruel world and the good die young."

Ruth Atkins tried not to listen to the words. She also tried not to turn around and stare at the speaker.

"I mean," the woman continued, "I wouldn't let my boy be a cop."

Finally, Ruth recognized the speaker and understood the shrill speculation. Her boy, Ruth knew, was unemployed and lived at home, at the age of fifty.

"And, I can't believe that now they allow women to be police officers. Why, in my day…"

Ruth turned around and glared.

The older woman smirked. "Well, let's just say that if I needed someone to protect me, I'd sure expect the cop who showed up to at least be taller than I am."

A swoosh of air escaped from between Ruth's teeth as she turned back to face the minister and listen to his eulogy. Eventually, her breathing returned to normal. She'd attended more than one anger-management session during the two years since she joined the police department. The department would be relieved to know the time had been well spent.

Once she had her breathing under control, Ruth stood, made her way to the aisle of the church and headed for the ladies' restroom where she leaned against the wall and closed her eyes. *The sixth cop in ten years. The fourth in the last two years.*

Jose Santos, a veteran of the police force for twenty-five years, beloved father of five, had hesitated when faced with shooting the car thief who palled around with his only daughter.

Two families destroyed: Jose's and the single mother who raised the shooter—a fifteen-year-old boy.

Jose's wife was burying her husband. Ruth was still looking for hers. In Ruth's case, there was no closure. Dustin was still listed as missing. No justice. Gracia Santos, Jose's wife, knew the murderer, could look the boy in the face and cry for justice.

But instead, Gracia, a Christian, cried for *both* her husband and the teenager.

Ruth had no compassion for the family of those who murdered her husband. She blamed the Santellises, and they were evil. Ruth would not, could not, shed a tear for the death of the two Santellis boys she blamed for Dustin's disappearance. They'd been shot just a year ago on the front steps of a Phoenix jail, and Ruth had been glad.

Glad!

Nothing would change Ruth's mind about that, not even the sound of "Amazing Grace" reverberating from the main auditorium. She opened her eyes hearing the bathroom door open. A face peeked around the corner.

"You okay?" Rosa Packard asked.

"I just need a moment. Really."

Rosa nodded before retreating, the way a best friend should.

Walking to the sink, Ruth grabbed a few hand towels and dabbed at her eyes. Fine time to have a pity party. The whole world, well, at least everyone at the Fifth Street Church, would know she'd been crying in the bathroom.

Last time she'd cried in this bathroom had been eight years ago. At only twenty, and with only twenty minutes to go until she walked down the aisle and said "I Do" to the love of her life, she'd stood in this very place and wept.

Not because she was sad, oh, no, but because she was about to enter the fairy-tale life she'd dreamed of. She was marrying a good man; she was going to have a good life.

And she had, for five years.

She'd married a man who was the antithesis of her father. She married a hero. This had been his church. It had also been Jose's. Her best friends Rosa and Sam Packard attended. For the last few months, Ruth and her daughter had accompanied them. Bible Study with Sam on Wednesday nights was becoming habit. And the new minister, Steve Dawson, seemed to direct some of his sermons right at her—usually the message had to do with forgiveness.

Well, she wasn't ready for that, not when it came to Dustin, but she was learning about Jesus, learning to pray, learning about this grace thing and *thinking* about being baptized.

The door opened again and Rosa poked her head in. "Ruthie, the service is almost over. People will be heading this way soon."

"Thanks." One last sniff, and Ruth followed Rosa into the auditorium and sat down.

Rosa patted Ruth's knee, a motherly touch, a needed touch, a touch that said *I'm here for you.*

Heads were bowed for the final prayer, and afterward Ruth joined the long line to say a final goodbye to Jose. His family stood by the casket accepting condolences. Or at least that's what Ruth thought they were doing.

"Thank you for coming." Gracia took Ruth's hand. Her hair was a curious mixture of black and red. She stood about a foot shorter than her children. Yet, she clearly was in charge. "My husband said you changed his mind about female cops. He so admired you for stepping up to the plate after Dustin disappeared. We pray every day for your family, for your loss."

"Thank you." Before Ruth had time to say anything else, to do what she'd intended and offer some platitude to help the woman cope, she was gently nudged aside by the person standing behind her.

Trying to shake off the gloom, Ruth stepped out into the August heat and hurried to her car. Clad in black slacks, a black shirt and black cotton jacket, she felt the full weight of the Arizona sun. Black was not the color for summer, as most of the mourners had proven by *not* wearing what Ruth's mother had deemed appropriate.

Ruth had first put on her dress uniform, a sign of respect *all* the other Gila City officers had followed. Then, she'd taken it off. She'd probably receive a reprimand from the captain. But, the captain would no doubt be pleased she'd made it to this funeral. She'd missed the last two. Now her only goal was to make it to her car without any more scenes.

She didn't want to be a cop mourning a cop.

Ruth had barely touched her key to the ignition when her cell phone vibrated. Ricky Mason, onetime classmate, onetime boyfriend, full-time reporter for the *Gila City Gazette*, clamored from the other end. Excitement took his naturally tenor voice up to an unnatural soprano. She held the phone away from her ear and in between an annoying amount of static caught the words *shed, Santellis, body.*

TWO

"Whoa, slow down, take a breath," Ruth advised. "What about a body?"

"Are you sitting down?" Ricky's words were rushed, a bit higher pitched than usual.

"I'm sitting down." Ruth told him. "I'm in the car, outside of Jose's funeral."

"Boy, that's where I should be, was supposed to be, but this is way more important—"

"Tell me about the body!" Ruth's keys fell to the floorboard. "What body?"

"They won't let me close yet, but I'm here at Eric Santellis's place—"

"The old cabin in Broken Bones? What are you doing out in Broken Bones?"

"When a Santellis calls in a dead body, boy, you know there's a story. I'm here in his kitchen—it's a mess—and waiting for the go-ahead to take some pictures, ask some questions. Right now they're not letting anyone close."

"You're kidding? Eric Santellis is back? He reported a dead body? Is it Dustin?" The words tumbled from her mouth even as her brain went into overdrive.

Dustin's cruiser had been found on Prospector's Way, the same road as the Santellis cabin.

"Look, I've only been here about fifteen minutes. I'm dating the girl who's working at the sheriff's office here, and she clued me in. That's not to be shared, by the way. They're annoyed I showed up. Eric—boy does he look like a Santellis—is in the living room. He's not talking, but he sure knows how to glare. Anyhow, he found a body this afternoon and called it in."

"I'm on my way. Call me if you find out anything."

"What and cause a wreck? I'll fill you in when you get here."

Ruth hurried out of her vehicle, got down on her hands and knees and fished her keys out from under the driver's side seat. She almost dropped them again, her hands were shaking so badly.

She aimed her small SUV toward Broken Bones and hit the speed dial on her cell phone and let her mother know she'd be late and to go pick up Megan from the babysitter.

I'm not ready for this.

Ruth clutched the cell phone. She should make one more call to a fellow police officer. She should call Sam Packard, her husband's best friend. Instead, her hand inched toward the car's radio. Dare she listen to hear if the news was reporting anything about a body found on Prospector's Way?

No, it was too soon. And if Ricky wasn't privy to information, neither were other reporters.

Oh, this was hard. She'd prayed for closure, and now that it was almost here all she felt was dread. Dread! She hated to admit it, but there'd always been this tiny germ of hope that Dustin would someday be discovered leading a secret life in some small community in Mexico. Amnesia. It would be amnesia.

Well, it could happen!

She turned onto the two-lane highway and got stuck behind a tractor trailer. The slow-moving vehicle gave her way too much time to think. Why had Eric Santellis returned to Arizona? He'd dropped off the earth after he'd gotten out of prison. Rosa said he'd gone looking for his sister. Ruth wished he'd stayed missing.

Leaving Gila City limits behind, Ruth entered a dirt road that jutted to the left and went a good two, three miles before introducing travelers to a type of one-horse town still alive and well in Arizona. She'd lived here for a few years back during her childhood. She remembered her mother cleaning houses to make a living, her father spending time in bars and in jail, and she remembered sleeping on a brown, smelly couch because there had only been one bedroom in the small house.

Broken Bones had thrived in the late 1800s; now it catered to an iffy tourist crowd and a dedicated modern-day gold prospectors crowd, most of whom stayed year-round.

By checking the dashboard clock, Ruth knew it had taken almost an hour to travel from the Fifth Street Church all the way to the Santellises' cabin.

It felt like forever.

The small SUV parked in front of the cabin blocked the entryway, and took up more room than necessary. The woman, slight of build and dressed in black, strode confidently to the door. She didn't knock. She opened the door and stepped in, zeroing in on Eric. The reporter started forward, took one look at both the woman and Eric and settled back to wait.

Small-town justice was an entity in itself. No doubt Officer Ruth Atkins figured any Santellis with a body in his shed would have news about the body she most wanted to find: her husband.

Eric had seen her in court all those months ago. On his behalf, in a halting voice, she outlined the investigation she'd been involved in and how she'd investigated the policeman who actually committed the murder Eric went to prison for. Of all who'd testified on his behalf, she was the only one who did it without a hint of compassion. It seemed that his last name, in her opinion, was enough to warrant a life sentence in Florence Prison. But, she was a cop through and through, as her husband had been, and she would testify truthfully, even if it broke her heart.

He felt guilty just looking at her and wondering which family member was responsible for making her a widow.

She stood, hands on her hips, with a Don't-you-dare-mess-with-me look in her red-rimmed eyes, and stated, "So, you found a body?"

"I did."

"Is it my husband?"

This he hadn't expected. For the last few hours his place had been an open-door invitation to both law enforcement and the medical field. The term *female remains* had been bantered around so often it sounded like a refrain from a rap song.

"No, the remains are female."

"I just found out." This was from the reporter who'd

been banned from the shed. Now at least Eric knew who the snitch was.

"It's a middle-aged woman, probably dead about six months," Eric said. "Whoever put her in the shed didn't really try to hide her. She was buried under clothes."

Ruth seemed to deflate but only for a moment. Then, she raised an eyebrow. Eric knew she was thinking the Santellises would be a bit more thorough, a bit more cruel.

Sheriff Mallery stomped into the room and frowned at Ruth. "What are you doing here?"

"I heard you had a body."

"Well, great guns, the news has probably made it to the moon by now." He motioned to Ricky. "You might as well head over there, don't touch anything and make sure to get the facts right." Ricky didn't need a second invitation. Ruth didn't even wait for one.

Mallery headed outside, leaving Eric alone with the ghosts of his ancestors both present and past. Not the position Eric wanted, so he slowly followed them. They had the shed's door propped open. August, in Arizona, was bad enough, hot enough. Add the stench of a dead body to the sweltering air and suddenly Siberia looked pretty inviting.

Every few minutes someone would exit and someone else would return. The coroner, annoyed at the chaos, threatened dire consequences should any feet stray too close to his victim and contaminate the area.

Eric leaned against the door frame and watched as Ricky displayed the unique ability of being able to write both in a cramped place and in the dark. Ruth hovered at Ricky's elbow. "It's a woman," she whispered in his ear.

"Duh," he responded.

Friendship, even in the worst of locales. Eric missed it, wanted it and didn't dare pursue it out here in the real world. The people he'd befriended in the past had a way of getting hurt—sometimes fatally.

Two deputies were busy moving boxes away from the corpse. Eric stayed on the stairs by the door. He could see everything and everybody. The coroner stood after a moment and said, "We can take a break now. I'll call dispatch and get the CSI guys out here."

The cops moving stuff sighed in relief. It was crowded, hot and dark in the shed. Compared to the smell, those were the good qualities. One of the cops put down the basket he'd just picked up. It teetered on the edge and fell to the ground with a thump only made louder by the self-imposed silence of the people in the shed.

At that moment, more than anything, Eric wished he'd remained on the porch, because when the coroner started packing his medical bag and the basket fell over, Eric spotted another hand.

THREE

Ricky, the reporter, got so excited he dropped his pen. The two deputies froze, probably fearful lest they move something and find yet another body. The coroner simply reopened his medical bag and waited for the deputies to snap out of their stupor and clear the way.

Eric watched Ruth. She didn't make a sound. The heat from the shed seemed to cloy as the players in this no-win game waited to see what would happen next. It reminded Eric of prison, of being in a place he couldn't breathe, a place with no soul. The smell of death, human sorrow and just plain wrongness, intensified. Although no one acknowledged the feeling, they all recognized it.

Sheriff Mallery finally snapped his fingers and barked at his deputies, "Well, you two just gonna stand there?"

Suddenly Ruth and Ricky were both pushed back as the need to maneuver boxes and clear the area became frenzied. Ricky obviously knew his job. He blended into the shadows. Ruth stumbled forward, her hand stretched out, her mouth a silent "0" of what? Fear? Shock? Disbelief? The deputies got busy and the hand became an arm, a torso, legs, a complete corpse.

From Eric's vantage point, he could tell this body had been a dead body longer than the woman's. The black slithery look was missing because there was no tissue left to rot. Only dingy brown bone remained. This corpse hadn't preferred the pink, flowered polyester of the first corpse. No, this corpse dressed a bit more conservatively, a bit more dignified.

But police uniforms, like pink polyester pantsuits, were meant to last.

Doctor Winters nodded in Ruth's direction and took on the same snappish tone the sheriff had just used. "Get her out of here."

"Nooo," Ruth keened.

The deputies didn't move; Ricky didn't move; the sheriff didn't move. The coroner was already on his knees in front of body number two. The white-haired doctor frowned. Shaking his head at what he knew to be a bad decision, Eric entered the shed and grabbed Ruth by the elbow. "Let's go back to the cabin."

"I need to see—"

"They'll work faster if you're not here. You're making them nervous."

Ruth glanced at the two deputies who were now both still—again. Nervous didn't begin to describe the looks on their faces. "Go, Ruthie," Ricky urged. "I'll tell you everything. I won't leave out a thing."

Her knees crumpled, and Eric held her upright. He moved her toward the open door. The top of her head came to his chest. It would have been easier to pick her up and carry her, but if he knew anything about this woman, it was that she wouldn't want to show weakness at this time. The sheriff moved aside to let them pass. He didn't offer to help. He didn't offer condolences or advice, either. He followed them out into the semifresh air and made a phone call. Doctor Winters did the same.

Eric had too much on his mind to even attempt to eavesdrop, though he was tempted. And each heavy step gave him time to think. *Two bodies! There are two bodies in my shed.* Maybe he should have waited before calling the authorities. This sheriff inspired about as much confidence as a used-car salesman. *Two bodies!* Helping Ruth across the front yard, up onto the porch, into the house and finally to the couch, he couldn't help but shake his head. *Two bodies and one of them belongs to her!*

He fetched a bottled water from the tiny kitchen, laid it at her feet and waited a moment to see what she'd do.

Nothing. She slumped forward instead of back. Her hands crossed her chest as if holding something— probably pain—inside. Her hair cascaded down and almost touched the floor. This was the first time he'd seen her in civilian clothes, not that black counted as a good first impression.

When the court had vacated Eric's conviction, and later during the trial of Cliff Handley's partners, Ruth had been in attendance, always wearing her police uniform. She'd also worn her hair in a braid that hid the fact that she had a rich, red, luxurious mane.

He went outside, found the same spot for phone reception he'd discovered earlier and called Rosa's cell. It was fifty-fifty he'd get through. Sam and Rosa would be at the other police officer's funeral. Eric couldn't remember the man's name, but he remembered how the man died. He'd been shot by a fifteen-year-old trying to steal a car. The news stations kept mentioning the kid's age, as if crime was reserved for adults. The residents of Gila City were shocked. Eric wished he could be shocked, but in his world, fifteen-year-olds knew more about guns than they did about skateboards.

Which is why he wanted to change his world.

He'd chosen Broken Bones because he wanted out of that life, that media circus. Yeah, right, as if he could be that lucky. That world had obviously followed him. No, not followed but preceded, giving him a proverbial Santellis welcome—You can run but you can't hide.

Rosa picked up after just two rings. "Packard here!"

He almost mentioned how he couldn't seem to get used to her new surname, but the timing wasn't right. Banter between him and his last remaining friend was strained, to say the least, mostly on his side. "I think you need to come out here. I found a body earlier, called it in and wound up with quite a few guests."

"Who'd you find?"

"First body was a female. Second body is wearing a police uniform. The bad news is Ruth is here."

"Second body? Police officer? Oh, don't tell me."

"I'm telling you."

"We'll be right there."

He went back in and sat on the floor. The couch was big enough for two, but he doubted Ruth would appreciate sharing with him—with the brother of the possible, probable, killer. She most likely figured he could tell her which sibling claimed guilt: Tony? Sardi? Kenny?

Of course, the murderer might not be one of his brothers. It could also very well be his brother-in-law. Until just over a year ago, Eddie Graham ran the Santellis Used-Car Lot in Gila City, barely thirty miles away.

Eric again shook his head. Currently, Eddie was doing a dime in Perryville Prison. Word had it he was happy there, that he didn't want to leave. Mary Graham, Eric's missing sister, had a temper. Her eight-year-old had gotten into his father's stash, digested some and had to be hospitalized. So now Eddie was in jail and his newest tattoo probably read I'm Too Scared of My Wife and Her Brothers To Move Back Home. Of course, now that Tony and Sardi were dead and Kenny missing, Eddie might reconsider parole. Maybe that's why Mary and her son were hiding.

The first thing Eric had done, after being released from prison, was get the electricity turned on out here in nowhereland, and then he spent some time looking for his sister, looking for the one piece of his life that might still need him as much as he needed it. Mary had vanished, and in some ways, he was grateful to know she was out of the life, out of the media's spotlight and maybe safe. He'd gone to Italy, to relatives he'd never met. So, even if the female had died within the last three months, Eric still had an alibi for much of it.

Thumps came from outside. Then came the sound of a highly agitated sheriff. This investigation bordered on the archaic. The effort to keep the area clean encouraged one mishap after the other. Good thing he'd already accepted that he lived in a fixer-upper, otherwise he'd be hard-pressed to keep the Santellis temper in check.

The damages were to be expected. Tender loving care would not have been in the vocabulary of the grandfather who'd left Eric the cabin. The fact that the place was in any decent shape at all could be credited to his sister. Mary and Eddie had lived in the cabin just after they'd married, and Eddie drove the sixty miles to his job at the Santellis Used-Car Lot in Gila City. Four years later, once their son, Justin, turned two, Mary insisted on moving back to Phoenix. She wanted to be close to doctors, stores, etc.

For the last eight years, the cabin had been deserted. Well, deserted except for Jane Doe and what was probably Dustin Atkins.

"Tell me how he died?" Ruth's words interrupted his thoughts.

He felt pathetically grateful to leave the images of the past, of his sister, his grandfather, his life, and focus on Ruth. She no longer bowed her head. Hair streamed in her face, obscuring most of her features but not hiding the fact that she'd been crying and hard. No woman he knew could cry that hard and keep silent.

His sister, Mary, wailed. Rosa was a gasper. He'd never seen his mother cry. Maybe she did it in secret, or maybe by the time he'd been old enough to notice, she'd forgotten how.

"I don't know how he died. I was in prison."

"Somebody would have told you."

"Right, I had so many visitors. That came up in court, remember?"

"How do you think he wound up in your shed?"

"Just my bad luck," Eric muttered.

"What?"

"It's just my incredibly bad luck. If one of my brothers murdered your husband, of course, they'd leave him in my shed. It's not like I can ever hope to break free of their doings."

"Did he make one of them angry?"

"How should I know?"

"Were they dealing drugs out of this house?"

"I'm gonna say no."

"What makes you say that?"

"The amount of dust and debris I've shoveled out. And if they had been dealing drugs from here, they'd have had a working stove and refrigerator. The windows would have been covered. Yes, even here in the middle of nowhere. Plus, there'd have been a chemical smell. There'd have been something tangible left behind, be it a broken propane canister, lithium batteries or rubber gloves."

"Maybe they cleaned up?"

"Yeah, right. They'd leave dead bodies but carry away the drug paraphernalia. No, the dirt was two inches deep."

"It's Dustin. I know it's him."

"I think so, too," Eric said.

"I think so three." Ricky the reporter stood in the cabin's doorway.

Eric almost stood up, almost shouted that now was not the time or place for any attempt at humor, but the look on Ruth's face stopped him.

"Have they said anything?" she asked.

"Boy, they've bantered his name around enough, but no one's willing to commit. They just kicked me out." He sounded indignant.

Eric was pretty amazed they'd let Ricky stay for so long, but then again, Eric had watched as Ricky the ace reporter melted into the shadows of a crime scene.

Walking to the doorway and nudging Ricky aside, Eric stared at his very popular shed. "Why'd they finally kick you out?"

Eric turned in time to catch a look passing between his guests. Finally, Ricky came clean. "They're saying the woman's only been dead about two to three months. So, Eric, you are a suspect. And they're saying Dustin didn't die in the shed. Somebody moved him and fairly recently."

FOUR

"Why would somebody move him?" Eric asked himself, a little too loudly. "And not move the female?"

"I don't know," Ruth answered. She stood up and paced. There was plenty of room since the only pieces of furniture in his living room were a lamp balanced on a crate in the corner, a couch with the stuffing coming out of one side and a coffee table made from an old door.

Eric thought the place perfect: secluded. He had everything he needed. More than the grandfather who'd left him the land. Eric even had electricity. He'd called and arranged to have it turned on before he arrived. But except for the lamp and the refrigerator, he didn't need the voltage. Maybe he should get rid of the lamp. All it did was remind Eric of how much work there was to do.

Ruth muttered, "He died somewhere else, and they moved him? Why?"

Ricky managed to restore a shred of respect to his profession, at least in Eric's opinion—and Eric despised reporters. He actually came up with a feasible supposition. "To frame you," he said, looking at Eric.

"That's pretty stupid since I was probably in jail when he bit the dust and travelling in Italy when she did."

"Maybe whoever moved them didn't know you'd been in prison," Ricky said.

"Right," Eric agreed. "Maybe whoever moved them has been buried under a rock for the last three years."

"Maybe whoever moved them didn't care which Santellis got blamed," Ruth guessed.

"What do you mean by that?" Eric asked. "You think my sister, Mary, might have—"

"I'm thinking more of your younger brother Kenny." Ruth stopped pacing and stared out the front door. The action by the shed reminded Eric of ants scurrying in and out of the nest.

Eric shook his head. "Kenny won't set foot near this place. He has a bounty on his head."

"I agree," Ricky said. "Besides, why move them for Kenny to find. He'd never have called them in. He'd have torched the shed to get rid of the smell and the evidence."

Ruth looked a little ill.

"You have the right to be sick at all this," Ricky said gently, "but all we're doing right now is supposing. We're even supposing the body is Dustin's."

"It's Dustin," Ruth said.

"Who else could it be?" Eric agreed.

"No other cop is missing." She started pacing again, this time with the quick, jerky motions of someone who was highly agitated. "But why was he in Broken Bones? It's not our jurisdiction—"

"Why are you in Broken Bones?" Eric asked. "It's not your jurisdiction."

She glared. "I got a call. You know that."

"Right, you got a call. Probably the same thing happened to Dustin. For some reason, be it a call, a hunch, whatever, he wound up here on Prospector's Way."

"Maybe he was looking into your brothers' involvement in the drug trade."

"That I believe, but they weren't working out of this cabin. It's mine. I told them to stay away."

"And they'd listen to you?"

"Yes."

Something flickered in her eyes—briefly replacing the sorrow—and clear enough to let Eric know she neither believed or trusted him.

He'd feel the same way if their roles were reversed.

This time she stopped by a window so dirty there were only a few streaks of cleanliness. She pointed outside, to where the road would be, and demanded, "Why would he be on this road?"

"Because this isn't the only cabin," Eric guessed.

She bent and stared out the smudge. "I hate this road, always did." She turned and glared at him. "What else were your brothers involved in?"

"You're a cop. You probably know more of their activities than I do. The only other person who might know is my father."

"Yano? I thought he died."

"He's has Alzheimer's. Right now he's in assisted living. Half the time, he doesn't even know when I'm there."

"He should be in prison," she said snidely.

Eric thought the same thing. And the part of him that still craved his father's acceptance, his father's love, thought that at least in prison the old man wouldn't be alone. Kenny was missing, Mary and her boy, Justin, were missing. Mom had died years ago. Tony and Sardi were dead, and if Yano's daughter-in-laws were smart, they'd remarry, have the new hubbies adopt the children and erase the Santellis name from all documentation.

"Off the top of your head, what else were your brothers involved in?"

"Prostitution. Money laundering. Chop shops. Extortion." He could have gone on, but the sheriff came in, gave Eric a dirty look, glanced back outside at the sound of more cars arriving and said, "Mrs. Atkins, you might want to wait outside. You have no idea how much he's involved."

"It's *Officer* Atkins, and since this man was in prison when Dustin disappeared, I'd say his alibi is airtight." Ruth had no idea why she defended Eric. Ricky had been right. He looked like a Santellis—somewhat. Maybe it was the *somewhat* that swayed her. The men in that family were all solid, dark, walking refrigerators who crushed what got in their way and never smiled. Eric had already shed his prison weight—not the muscles— and was a slender dark man who lived in a hovel and never smiled.

"We will connect him to the murders," the sheriff argued.

"No, you won't," came a voice from the doorway. "He didn't have to call the bodies in. He could have simply dug their graves a little deeper and forgotten about them." Rosa Packard, still wearing her dress blues from the funeral—stretched tight due to pregnancy—stepped into the room followed by her husband, Sam, and Steve Dawson, the preacher who had just done Jose's funeral service.

Sam Packard nodded at Eric but went straight to Ruth, sat down next to her on the couch and wrapped his arms around her. For a moment, Ruth lost herself. She knew this man, had known him for years. She'd been two years behind Dustin and Sam in school and had envied their friendship. They'd done almost everything together: Boy Scouts, high-school baseball team and finally Sam had been the best man at Ruth and Dustin's wedding. In a pinch, he even babysat Megan.

When Sam joined the police force, he and Dustin had been partners—until Dustin's disappearance. When Ruth decided to join the police force—good money, good benefits, good way to keep active the investigation into Dustin's disappearance, Sam had been there to tell her it was a bad idea and later to help her learn to shoot a gun.

She began to train, get in shape, and after two months she earned her badge. A year later, instead of Dustin, Ruth served as Sam's partner on the Gila City police force. Then, yet another year passed, and Ruth walked down the aisle at Rosa and Sam's wedding. She'd fought back tears because Dustin deserved to be at his best friend's side. He deserved the chance to tell Sam that marriage meant bad breath in the morning and long kisses goodbye. Marriage meant fighting over whether or not to put mushrooms in the gravy and going to bed before you're tired just so you can go to bed at the same time. Marriage meant watching the stick turn blue together and knowing that in nine months there'd be cries in the middle of the night and a little baby that looked like daddy.

A fairy tale.

She cried at Sam's wedding because she was so very happy for Sam, and so very unhappy without Dustin.

Why were all these thoughts surfacing now? Was it because any tiny shred of hope concerning Dustin was probably about to dissolve? Staring across the room, she studied Eric Santellis. He sat next to Rosa and gazed at her intently. They spoke in low intimate tones.

Next to Ruth, Sam offered platitudes. Then, the minister offered more, and all the while, Rosa and Eric whispered about his big brothers.

His brothers.

If they weren't already dead...

"Did you know Eric had moved here?" Ruth shifted, freeing herself from the comfort of Sam's arms.

"Yes," Sam admitted. "He called Rosa last week."

"Why didn't you tell me?"

"Never seemed like the right time. Jose died Monday night, and, well, okay, I kept finding reasons to put off telling you."

"That's so lame. You knew I'd want to know about Eric *Santellis* moving to Broken Bones, taking up residence in this cabin, *on this road.*"

Sam took one of Ruth's hands and explained to Steve. "This is the road where they found Dustin's cruiser. From the beginning, the Santellises were suspects. We searched for miles. I know we went inside that shed. If his body was there, back then, we'd have found it."

"They're saying his body was moved," Ruth mumbled.

The minister took Ruth's other hand. "It might not be Dustin."

"It's Dustin," Eric stated. "Who else could it be?"

"Someone from Phoenix," Sam guessed, looking at Eric. "Your family made plenty of enemies there. This would be a perfect place to hide a body."

"My brothers would never have left a body, make that bodies, so exposed that anyone willing to move a box or a laundry basket would stumble over them."

"True," Rosa agreed.

"And he's wearing a uniform," Ruth muttered.

"You saw it?" Sam asked.

Ruth nodded.

"What's Mallery thinking?" Sam's annoyance was obvious. "That crime scene is probably so trampled nothing is left." He looked at Eric. "What about the first body? The one you called in?"

"It's a woman. She's wearing pink polyester. She hasn't been in there long. She still has features."

"You know," Rosa said slowly, "Eric made a good point. His brothers would have buried the bodies so deep only a steam shovel could have unearthed them."

"Maybe they were in a hurry," the minister said. Dawson had only been in Gila City for eight months. Eric's older brothers died before his arrival. For the past few months, the Santellis name had lost much of its luster. No one was left to enforce the reputation. It amazed Ruth how quickly the public forgot, how fickle were their memories, how enhanced hers was—at least when it came to the Santellises and what they'd done in Gila City and Broken Bones. She really hadn't needed to ask Eric about their other vices. She'd known all about them…every cop did, every cop wanted to bring the family down.

And Rosa *had*. Yet she and Eric Santellis called each other friend. Maybe Ruth could have forgiven Eric if he'd moved some place like Miami or New York City—some place far, far away.

"Ma'am?" It was one of the two deputies. "Sheriff said

to show this to you." He had a Ziploc baggy in his hand. "See if the number belonged to your husband."

Ruth took what he offered and almost dropped it. Then, she grasped it so tightly that the edges dug into her palm leaving red indentations. When she finally opened her hand and stared at the badge, she felt almost surprised by how ordinary it looked. It hadn't tarnished; Dustin would be pleased. He shone the thing every morning. And it was Dustin's badge. It bore his number and traces of his blood.

Sam jumped up, pushed past the deputy and ran across the yard. Numbly, Ruth followed, stood on the porch, suddenly afraid to go any farther, and listened. Rosa and Eric soon joined her. Rosa took her hand and squeezed. "I'm so, so sorry. So sorry."

Numb, Ruth swallowed back the tears and squeezed in return. The Santellises had been responsible for the death of Rosa's parents and brother. If anyone understood Ruth's pain, her sorrow, it would be her best friend, Rosa.

A loud confrontation began inside the shed. Ruth recognized Sam's shouts. Words like *proper procedure, common sense* and *idiot* punctuated the air. Then, it got quiet. Next, those waiting on the porch were privy to a higher-pitched shout. Ruth guessed it to be Sheriff Mallery—a man she'd bugged off and on for the last two years, always trying to find out some info on her husband. He delivered the final blow. "…last one to see her alive."

The deputy who'd delivered the badge looked relieved not to be part of the shed's crowd. The door to the shed opened, and the other deputy hurried toward the porch. Sam was on his heels.

"Ma'am?" the deputy said.

Ruth gripped a porch rail, but the cop wasn't talking to her. He was addressing Rosa.

"Yes."

"Sheriff wants you to come to the shed. He thinks you can help with the other body."

Rosa's eyebrows drew together. One hand dropped to her stomach. "Me? Are you sure he meant me?"

"I'm sure."

"Honey—" Sam's teeth were clinched "—don't worry, there's no way they can tie you to this crime."

Rosa blanched. One hand dropped to her stomach. "Sam, we overhead some of what the sheriff said. What's going on?"

"Yes, Sam, what's going on?" Ruth looked from the deputy to Sam to Rosa and took a step back.

FIVE

It was the preliminary identification of the pink-clad woman as Lucille Damaris Straus that ended any hope Eric had of settling in quietly at Broken Bones. The same identification moved Rosa to first place on the list of suspects. The sheriff made the necessary phone calls and government intervention arrived in the form of state agencies and the FBI.

Rosa and Sam were hustled off to who knows where. Eric, Ricky, the minister and Ruth were ordered to stay in the cabin. At first, they'd all headed for the porch, curiosity so tangible it almost pushed them. After a few stern looks, they retreated inside. Then, carefully, Eric headed for the porch and a rocker. Ruth followed, taking the second rocker.

For Eric, sitting still and simply observing was not a hardship. He'd spent a lifetime learning how to be seen and not heard. It had saved his hide more than once both growing up in the Santellis family and later while surviving in prison. If what he was observing now was true, Ruth didn't know how to sit still. White-knuckled hands clutched the armrests of the rocking chair. Impatient feet tapped a beat that threatened to dance off the porch. Tenaciously balanced on the edge of the seat, she was poised for flight but shackled by her belief in the system.

A belief he didn't share. "You do know that Rosa couldn't possibly be involved in this?"

She looked at him, blinked and finally settled into the chair. "I—I—I don't know what to think. I'll wait—"

"Did you ever meet Lucy?"

She stared at him, as if surprised everyday conversation was possible. Her feet slowed their dance and her knuckles relaxed. "No, I think Rosa had already gotten her off the street by the time I joined the force. And, if I ran across her before that, I'd not have thought twice."

Gila City and Broken Bones had their quota of the homeless, thanks to the lack of winter. Eric knew Ruth to be an Arizona native, which meant acclimated to the sight of men and women pushing shopping carts loaded with an odd assortment of belongings. "If I remember correctly," Eric said, "she was mentally ill."

Ruth nodded, but didn't respond.

"I wonder how she wound up in my shed. Rosa said something about Lucy having a rough childhood…."

A man wearing a suit much too dignified for the middle of a desert crime scene walked toward the porch and called, "Mrs. Atkins. We'd like to show you something."

And she was gone, before Eric could convince her of Rosa's innocence, *of his innocence.*

Funny, she was the only doubter he wanted to convince.

He certainly felt no need to convince the barrage of officials who crowded into his living room. The minister was escorted home. Who knew where Ricky, the reporter, disappeared to? And the officials, convinced Eric not only knew how the bodies came to be in his shed but also who put them there, let him know that his contributions, or lack thereof, only angered them.

It didn't matter to them that Eric hadn't been to the cabin in a decade. It didn't matter to them that he had alibis. And, it didn't matter to them that other than serving time and later being exonerated, he had no criminal record.

All he could do was tell them the history of his family's cabin. His great-great-great-grandfather had built the cabin in the 1800s. His grandfather had left it to Eric. His sister and her husband had lived in it a decade ago. Yes, Rosa knew about the cabin. Yes, Rosa had been his sister's childhood friend. She'd been his teenage crush. His oldest brother was responsible for her brother's death. He'd hooked up with her during an undercover sting operation four years ago. They both worked on the side of good. Ten months ago, she, her husband, Ruth and a man named Mitch Williams proved Eric innocent of murder of the police officer he'd been working with. That's when he heard about Lucy Straus. He'd never met the woman. His story never changed. It couldn't. It was the truth.

A truth that didn't make the authorities any happier. They wanted to solve this case. It would be so much easier if they could tighten the noose around a Santellis neck.

They were willing to work all night to tie the knot. Eric's last thought, as he stretched out on the couch in his living room, his bed for now, was about how the local authorities were making it perfectly clear they'd settle for Rosa's neck instead of his.

* * *

The alarm rang at six. Eric didn't remember setting it, and for a moment, he contemplated getting a few more minutes shut-eye. That's when he heard the voices outside and the memory of yesterday's mess catapulted him off the couch and back to his front porch.

The door to the shed was open. Eric started toward it. The sheriff, looking as though he hadn't been to bed at all, stepped out and shook his head. Eric interpreted the look: I ask questions; I seldom answer them, and I don't know how to share.

After downing a bowl of cereal and brushing crumbs off the low-slung jeans he'd slept in, Eric decided to act as if this Saturday morning was like any other. He'd start checking for exterior and interior damage, start doing with the cabin what he'd be doing if the authorities weren't here. It's not as if they were including him in the investigation. Plus, maybe if he blended into the scenery, didn't appear so much an observer, they'd forget he was here, talk a bit more freely, and then he could figure out what they were doing with Rosa.

Before he could begin, James Winters's white Cadillac pulled up and the elderly doctor stepped out. Wisely, he avoided the shed and came toward Eric instead.

"Curiosity is a poor bedfellow," he said. "I didn't sleep all night. Feel like company?"

"Think they'll let you stay?"

"Sheriff owes me."

The doctor sat in the second rocker and tossed Eric a newspaper. "Thought you'd find this interesting."

Eric settled back into his chair and cringed. Friday's *Gila City Gazette*'s front-page headline screamed Mafia

Hit! The first few paragraphs focused on Lucille Damaris Straus, the pink-clad woman.

Ricky the reporter had gotten it right. Lucy had first come to the nation's attention last year when the truth about Cliff Handley, a Gila City native and a beloved police officer who lived a double life, was made public. Lucy, a homeless woman, had assisted in his arrest rather unwittingly. She'd loaned, for a price, her identity to Rosa. Using Lucy's name and social-security number, Rosa made a place for herself in Gila City and hunted down every person, every place, every move from Cliff's past. Her goal: to prove Eric innocent. She'd ferreted out details about Cliff Handley that not even he realized. Then Rosa had been arrested and her true identity revealed. She was a mere civilian determined to see justice done. But her arrest exposed the truth about both Cliff and Eric.

Cliff was a murderer; Eric was not.

Unfortunately, Lucy hadn't been around last year for Rosa to ceremoniously return her identification. And even more unfortunate was the general consensus that Rosa, who claimed not to have seen Lucy in all that time, most likely was the last person to see Lucy alive. Add to that the fact that Rosa's fingerprints were on some of Lucy's belongings and, for the authorities and press, the consensus easily turned into the questions *Did Rosa kill Lucy? And if so, why?*

Dustin Atkins got equal coverage. Pictures of his deserted squad car, found just a mile from Eric's cabin, looked sinister. A family photo of Dustin, Ruth and a little girl looked prime-time perfect. The piece on Dustin began with his dedication to keeping Gila City's youth off drugs; it ended with Ruth's new position on the police force and her dedication to not only ridding the streets of killers but also keeping her husband's case open.

Finally Eric turned the page and was treated to his own history—that of the Santellis crime family. He didn't need to read a word. They dealt drugs. Most had the word *Killer* tattooed on their forearms.

In Eric's opinion, the press needed to spend more time on the verifiable truth. Rosa was a cop, married to a cop and about to have a little cop. Nowadays, everything she did was by the book. Eric was a Santellis trying to start a new life. It didn't seem to matter to the press that innocents were intruded upon. It didn't matter to curious locals, either. Like the minivan of retirees who were slowly driving past his cabin. The couples, families and even the occasional single female who slowed down for a look felt like paparazzi. And every hour it got worse. Eric, and everyone else trying to keep the crime site intact, watched as a little-traveled road on Prospector's Way turned into a traffic jam. Only Doc seemed able to handle the deluge of people. He knew most of them. He returned greetings, asked one driver about the year of his BMW, claimed not to know anything about the bodies, *yet,* and advised the drivers to leave the policing to the police and go home.

A few brave souls yelled for Eric to sign their newspaper, which pretty much acted like a road map to the stars. Eric's home was becoming one of Arizona's seven wonders, a landmark destination ranked right up there with the Grand Canyon.

Sheriff Mallery growled every time the curious slowed down for a stare. Of course, Mallery had more than a passing interest in the traffic. His family owned the land adjacent to Eric's and had for as long as the Santellises had owned theirs. No doubt, until now, most of the town was unaware of the pitiful condition of the sheriff's younger brother's cabin. Old cars, trash, broken-down campers, you name it, littered the Mallery land. It looked much like the Santellis property—only now Eric intended to change that, clean up his land, make it livable.

After the first hour and with no slowdown of the deluge of cars, Mallery sent a deputy to ascertain the names of those who "belonged" on Prospector's Way. There were five cabins, two ranches and one permanent gold camp with a population of just over a hundred. It wouldn't be easy, but it was necessary to identify locals. That same deputy was now busy setting up road barriers. By late afternoon the traffic should return to normal.

Normal?

Nothing was normal for a Santellis.

Or maybe what Eric was witnessing now was normal for his family. In the last hour, he'd heard that Rosa's lawyer wanted her to have nothing to do with him; he'd heard that Dustin Atkins had been positively identified; and he'd heard that the only good Santellis was a dead Santellis.

He doubted the sheriff cared that he'd been overheard.

SIX

"I'm so sorry about your loss." It was the same woman who, in a grating voice, had tallied the death toll at Jose's funeral. It made sense she'd attend Dustin's funeral, too.

Some cop Ruth was. If a sketch artist were to ask what the speaker looked like, Ruth wouldn't be able to assist. Her blinding tears made it impossible to do anything but nod.

"Technically," the woman continued, "Dustin Atkins cannot be considered as the seventh to die in the line of duty but the third. He died well before Jose."

Died? It still sounded like a foreign word. Ruth had spent two years carefully saying *missing*. Now, thanks to dental records, Dustin had been positively identified on Saturday, and Ruth officially became a widow. They released his body on Monday. And here it was Thursday, just one week after Jose's service, and the Gila City police were once again saying goodbye to one of their own.

"Thank you for coming," Ruth said. She'd said the same thing to at least a hundred people.

"I wouldn't miss it," the woman said. "But I just can't believe the gall of some people." She looked at the back row of the church where Sam and Rosa sat. Without missing a beat, she continued, "That woman is bad news. How she became a police officer, I'll never know."

Ruth almost said *Two months at the police academy in Phoenix learning how to fight, shoot and handle dead bodies, that's how. Same as me.* But the woman didn't need to hear the words, wouldn't have heard them if Ruth had uttered them. No, the busybody prattled on, fascinated with her own theories, theories that were being bandied about by almost all the people who knew Rosa had been taken in for questioning.

Did Rosa kill Lucille Straus? And, if so, why?

What did the authorities know that they were keeping back even from her? Surely there had to be something more than fingerprints.

Guilt and suspicion wrapped their hands around Ruth's already broken heart. Rosa was her best friend, so much so that Ruth had planned to throw Rosa a baby shower in just a few months.

Who knew what would happen in the next few weeks? The suspicion and guilt didn't feel natural. It didn't feel right. Yet, the events of that morning replayed at the most inopportune times—like at funerals.

Ruth blinked away the tears. She had to regain control of herself. She couldn't lose it, couldn't keep reliving the day she'd been forced to accept his death.

Looking around the church, she found Megan right where she'd left her, sitting next to Grandma and Uncle Billy. Tears slid down the five-year-old's cheeks. Truthfully, Megan didn't remember the man Ruth referred to as Daddy. What Megan understood was that most of her friends had daddies and that daddies must be a wonderful thing.

Last night, Ruth sat Megan down and delicately explained that Rosa might somehow be in trouble.

Megan said, "Nope, not Miss Rosie."

Megan's allegiance to Rosa brought Rosa's fan club to three: Eric, Sam and Megan. No one else wholeheartedly bought into Rosa's innocence. The police were calling Rosa a person of interest. They found her so interesting she was put on leave until their investigation either found her innocent or found her even more interesting.

Ruth didn't know what to believe. She only knew that if Sam had been married to anyone else, he'd be sitting with her, on the other side of Megan and Uncle Billy, offering comfort, and being a best friend to Dustin one last time. Instead, Sam sat in the very last pew, next to Rosa, who looked ready to cry. Sam looked ready to hit something.

The police liaison started guiding the rest of the stragglers into the auditorium. Too bad he hadn't started ten minutes before the woman with the grating voice got hold of Ruth. Now Ruth had a headache along with heartache.

Entering the auditorium, she slipped into the pew and stared at the closed casket. Three pictures of Dustin sat on top of the American flag. One was of him, his parents and his brother Billy. Another, just of him, showed a cop proud of his uniform. The final portrait, of the family, showed Dustin with an arm around each of his girls: Ruth and Megan. Next to an elaborate array of flowers, a slide show played on a television set: Dustin during childhood and his teenage years, with parents who had gone ahead of him. Dustin going through the police academy, getting married, becoming a dad. The television faded to black and Steve Dawson led the prayer starting the memorial.

As the minister cited Romans and called Dustin one of God's servants, Ruth removed two wrinkled pages of notes from her purse. Last night, she'd written her last tribute to her husband. Once the minister finished his talk, Dustin's peers took their place behind the podium. One after another, five, ten, and even more, they spoke about Dustin's bravery, his even temper, his dedication to the force, his family, God. How much they missed him.

Ruth's throat closed—no way would she be able to go up front and stumble through her notes. The dam broke and tears spilled over.

Cops don't cry.

That's what she'd told herself at Jose's funeral. And she'd believed it. But today she wasn't a cop. No, today she was a widow, a single mother and feeling so alone.

Cops do cry.

She felt the arm go around her shoulder and leaned into its comfort. Sam Packard had taken his rightful place beside his best friend's widow.

"Two years," Ruth whispered.

"What?"

"I figured it out and wrote it down." She handed him the notes. "From childhood, the only time you and Dustin separated were those two years you served in the military."

Sam nodded and glanced over her words. "He had seniority over me in the police force because of those two years. He sure loved to remind me of that."

"Yup. He did."

"He stayed in Gila City because of you."

"Yup." Ruth always held that knowledge close to her heart. Dustin loved her and chose not to follow the military career he and Sam had planned during high school. Sam had been his best friend; Ruth had been his best girl, until Megan's birth had given him the privilege of having two best girls. "Oh, Sam," she whispered, "say it isn't so."

"I wish I could." He sounded choked up.

"How will I live without him?"

"The way you've been living without him for the last three years. You'll hold his memory close, and you'll know you're surrounded by good friends. You also know that God is with you. He won't leave you."

Sam had said much the same thing during the early days of Dustin's disappearance, and Ruth had shaken her head. Dustin had been faithful to God, and back then, to Ruth's mind, God hadn't been faithful to Dustin. She didn't shake her head today. Not with a church full of people who one after the other got behind the podium. Every single police officer and church friend mentioned Dustin's faith. Every single one, even those who didn't share his faith.

Sam left her side and walked to the front. Those who'd been whispering fell silent. Ruth bowed her head, and every word Sam uttered, she repeated. He managed to add almost every point she'd made in her notes and attributed them to her. He also mentioned how she was coming to know the God who meant so much to Dustin.

After the service, Jose's whole family surged forward to hug Ruth, pat Megan on the head and invite them to dinner. "You'll come to our house soon, for dinner," Gracia Santos said, "and bring your family."

"I don't know. Maybe if…"

"No maybes. We're widows together. You're not alone. We have God, and we have each other." Gracia's children, only a step behind their mother nodded. "That includes you, too, Sam Packard," Gracia said loudly. Sam had been gathering the pallbearers to the side, readying them for the drive to the cemetery. "You hear?" Gracia asserted.

"I hear," he acknowledged.

"And bring your wife." With that, Gracia looked at Ruth as if daring her to squabble.

Ruth nodded in what she hoped looked like noncommitment. She was outnumbered, no doubt. Jose's big happy family had always fascinated her. She'd been an only child born to a man who didn't deserve children. Dustin had been the second son born to two people who thought he hung the moon, and Ruth had always been grateful his parents hadn't had to deal with his disappearance. They died right after Megan was born.

Carolyn George, Ruth's mother, leaned against a wall with her eyes closed. This funeral made the second time Ruth was aware of that her mom had stepped foot inside a place of worship. The first had been Ruth's wedding.

"We're so sorry." The words jarred Ruth, returning her to the present. Mourners still waited to offer her emotional support. Phone numbers were pressed in Ruth's hand. Women hugged, and men shuffled to the unheard beat of "I don't know what to do or say." Interspersed between the church people were Dustin's police buddies and their families. Emotional support was not the goal, though. She heard, instead, "If anybody bothers you… If you just need drive-bys… If… If… If…"

When the line slowed down, Ruth sidled over. "Mom, are you all right? You look a bit overwhelmed."

"This is nothing like your father's funeral."

Darryl George, Ruth's father, didn't have any friends.

His buddies at the bar couldn't tear themselves away from the bottle long enough to come pay their condolences.

"Everyone loved Dustin," Ruth said instead.

"Yes, they did." Billy Atkins, Dustin's big brother, came up behind her. "It's time to go, Ruth." Billy guided the two women to the waiting limousine. Megan held his hand until he hustled her in next to her mother. Then, he went back to the car with the other pallbearers. The drive to the cemetery took twenty minutes. It should have taken five, but the line of cars looked unending.

"Your daddy was a hero," Ruth said to Megan.

So much a hero, the cemetery didn't have enough parking. A good number of people missed the final prayer before Dustin Atkins was lowered into the ground. They only got to see Megan carrying her daddy's flag back to the limo. Finally, the family returned to the funeral home where Ruth signed one final paper.

She'd just taken care of Dustin for the last time.

Twenty minutes later, she pulled into the driveway of the house she and Dustin had shared. Cars lined the streets of her neighborhood, spilling around the corner. Dustin's friends, *her friends,* were bringing food. Megan had the back door opened before the car completely stopped.

Ruth's mother could only utter, "Oh, my," as they crossed the lawn and finally entered the house to find a banquet of casseroles, fried chicken, chips, so much food they wouldn't need to cook for a week. And in the kitchen, there was Sam trying to find room in the refrigerator for some hard-boiled eggs while Rosa washed dishes at the sink.

Rosa was noticeably alone, even as her church friends patted her on the back and whispered encouragement.

Suspicion's cloak might as well have been colored bright red. It was clear that the community was not only doubtful as to her involvement in Dustin's murder, but also as to how Ruth might react to seeing Rosa in her kitchen.

"Miss Rosie," Megan cried, running over to her beloved friend. "You're here."

And that was when Ruth knew she hadn't just taken care of Dustin for the last time. She still had one more thing to do: find his killer.

SEVEN

Ruth's mother hustled the last visitor out the door just after nine o'clock, picked up her crochet and settled on the couch to watch a legal thriller rerun. Ruth changed out of her black clothes and a few minutes later she stood staring at the mounds of food littering her kitchen.

It would take them a year to make a dent in all this. She took a tentative step toward the table where bags of chips and a stack of canned goods waited. She looked around the kitchen for someplace different to set them, then put them back down. She couldn't do this, rearrange the food in the kitchen, act normally.

Where had this exhaustion come from? Burying her husband *today?* Finding her husband *last week?* Worrying about her husband the *last few years?* It was a good thing she'd learned to pray because prayer was the only thing that would give her any comfort tonight.

Three years of wondering was over. It was time to go on with "let go and let God" as Sam would say. First she wanted God to let her go find Dustin's killer. No, second she wanted God to let her go find Dustin's killer, first she wanted God to help her take good care of the daughter Dustin left behind.

Turning off the kitchen light, she tiptoed down the hall to check on Megan. The little girl had fallen asleep hours ago while the house still bustled with activity. Stuffed with the food and attention of those who loved her, she'd just plain worn out.

Ruth stood in Megan's doorway, listening to the gentle breathing, and then she headed out to the garage, to her office. Three years ago she'd moved her mother into Dustin's office, and Dustin's office out here. Back then, for a solid week, while her mother got to know Megan, Ruth had gone through each and every one of Dustin's notes, looking for information about the Santellises and writing everything in notebooks. She *knew* they were the murderers. Later, convinced there was nothing left to discover, she'd packed up his files and stored them in the crawl-space sized attic. She didn't need them anymore; she'd started taking her own notes on the Santellises.

Now was as good a time as any to open up the files that had been gathering dust for almost a year. It looked as though Rosa needed her, but this time it seemed that Rosa's plight had something to do with Dustin.

The last time she'd written anything down had been when she testified for Eric Santellis. Her testimony helped release him. She'd thrown up afterward.

Her mother opened the door that separated the garage from the laundry room. "Please don't tell me it's starting again."

"What?"

"You, the notebooks, the search for answers, this obsession with the Santellises and the town of Broken Bones." Carolyn gripped the door so hard, Ruth thought maybe her mother was about to faint.

"I need to know what happened."

"But Ruthie, some things are better left alone."

"Like what? The fact that someone moved Dustin's body, put it in a shed, next to another body that somehow wound up there, and now the local authorities think they can blame Rosa? I have six weeks of leave. I intend to find the murderer this time."

Her mother shook her head and slowly closed the door. How many times had Ruth seen the exact same move whenever her father was acting out? Mom had retreat down to a fine art. Not so Ruth. First, she pulled out the maps Dustin had kept of the area. He probably knew as much about the area as anyone. Some of Dustin's earliest maps were yellow-and-brown with age and looked as if a ten-year-old had made a pencil drawing. They showed the old mines, a small town, long-eradicated tunnels and only two roads. The latest map was a few years old and was not only in color but also glossy. There were quite a few more roads.

How had Dustin's body gotten to that shed? In the trunk of somebody's car? In a bag? From which direction? Closing her eyes, she could see the outskirts of Broken Bones as it was almost two decades ago when she lived there. It was a brown, ugly town that smelled like hot cement and sweat. A sign at the city limits boasted a population of just over five hundred.

She spent two years of her life in Broken Bones. Years that centered around a drab house, a lonely school, a bar, a sheriff's office and a grocery store—in that order. The house was as brown and ugly as the town. She'd attended Thomas T. Mallery Elementary School for third and fourth grades. Her one-and-only friend had been Ricky

Mason. Elizabeth Winters, Doc's wife, had been her third-grade teacher. When Ruth's mother worked late cleaning for the Winters family, Ruth saw what a family meal looked like. It's was Ruth's first introduction to the prayer before meals. Doc had always said it, and Mrs. Winters'd said "Amen."

Pictures, of the Winterses' grown children and their children, had lined their walls. A time line of family antiques filled the shelves. Ruth knew even in fourth grade that she wanted what the Winters had.

What she didn't want was what she had. Namely, a father who couldn't stay out of trouble and who preferred Axel's Bar to home. "Just going to town," Darryl George would tell his wife many an afternoon. "I'll pick up some milk." Sometimes, as if to prove his story, he'd take Ruth with him. A few times, he even remembered the milk. More often than not, he forgot about his daughter sitting there, outside the bar, waiting, on the sidewalk. Sometimes she still felt like that lonely, lost girl, picking herself up off the sideway and walking home, believing in the ghosts of Broken Bones the whole way.

The jail was another establishment Ruth knew well. True, she'd visited it plenty after Dustin disappeared, but she'd known it two decades earlier, as well. It was the only two-story building in Broken Bones. Two cells were upstairs. The main floor housed offices, a waiting room, booking room, etc. All the rooms the general public expected to see. The basement had one cell and storage.

Ruth's dad had always been upstairs. His crimes were enough to build his reputation as a petty criminal but not enough to warrant moving him to Florence or

Perryville Prison. He'd turn over in his grave now if he knew his daughter was an officer of the law.

"You need to go to bed." Her mother appeared again.

Ruth glanced down at the maps and at the file labeled Broken Bones. She hadn't even opened it. She'd been lost in her own history instead of Dustin's. "I hate Broken Bones," she whispered.

Carolyn nodded.

"And I hate that Dustin died there. Of all places, there."

Carolyn again nodded.

"Why did you stay with him?"

Carolyn didn't question who "him" was. Darryl George was a topic they avoided. Three years ago, just after Dustin went missing, Carolyn moved in with Ruth. It was a blessing for both of them. Ruth had a live-in babysitter, and Carolyn felt needed. The arrangement worked until Ruth brought up her father. The merest mention of his name sent her mother out the door. At first it was to the park down the street, but then as Ruth became bolder, and asked even more pointed questions, her mother increased the time and distance of her escapes. Still, all Ruth had to do was head for one of Carolyn's friend's houses.

Mom's face tightened. It was a look Ruth remembered well.

"Why did you stay with him? And why, whenever I ask you about our time spent in Broken Bones, do you leave and I have to find you?"

Carolyn started for the door.

"Don't do it. Don't walk out."

For a moment, Carolyn hesitated. She almost turned, almost said something, but before she could—

"Mom!" Megan's voice, a distant whine, interrupted whatever Carolyn might have been about to say. Ruth left her mother, the maps, the files, basically the clutter of her life, and headed for her daughter's room.

"You okay?"

The flyaway brown hair came from Dustin, so did the brown eyes and wide lips. Size and imagination came from Ruth. Megan, like Ruth, knew there really were monsters in the closet. Ruth's had been real. Its name had been Darryl George. With Megan, they were imaginary and had started back when Dustin stopped coming home, and Ruth took a full-time job. "It's so quiet," Megan complained, picking at the edge of her blanket. "I'm thinking about Daddy. And I'm alone."

"Grandma and I are both here. We were in the garage."

"You're not going to work tomorrow, are you?"

"No, not for a long time." No need to explain to a five-year-old the ins and outs of family emergency leave. Ruth was just grateful to have time to spend with her family, time to spend burying Dustin both physically and mentally.

"Will you sit in the chair?"

"Yes, I can do that."

Years ago, when Megan was a baby, Ruth would pick her up and rock her in the pale blue rocking chair. Sitting in that chair with a precious little daughter had made the exhaustion almost pleasurable. Not like today. Putting her feet on the floor instead of on the footstool, Ruth pushed herself back and forth while listening to her daughter breathe and to the sound of the television returning to life in the next room, her mother's room.

So, Carolyn was sticking around.

And Ruth needed to decide if she wanted to pursue this conversation on the day she buried her husband.

Some things needed to stay buried. Ruth was smart enough to believe that; she just didn't intend to allow it to happen.

EIGHT

The aroma of breakfast pulled Ruth from a sound sleep. Good thing, too, because if she'd slept in the rocker any longer, her neck would forever tilt at an awkward angle. After making sure Megan was still asleep, Ruth stumbled from the room and joined her mother in the kitchen.

Her mom hadn't prepared breakfast since her husband died. He'd always demanded she make him three pancakes, four slices of bacon, two pieces of toast and orange juice. For a man who didn't bring home a regular paycheck, sometimes his demands were unrealistic. But Ruth couldn't remember a morning her mother didn't make the breakfast.

Sitting down at the kitchen table, Ruth picked up a fork, examined it and asked, "You ready to talk?"

"No."

"Why are you making breakfast then?"

"Because I'm willing to change."

"What all are you going to change?"

"I've not completely decided. Right now I'm just changing my morning habits. I've always liked breakfast.

I let your father take that away from me, along with other things, and I need to get it, and them, back."

"Talk to me, Mom."

"I can't today, Ruthie. I need to think."

"Darryl's been dead for ten years. You've been changing ever since, for the better. What do you need to think about?"

"I need to think about the change in you." Mom plopped two pancakes on a plate and then set it in front of Ruth. "I'm thinking I made some wrong decisions." Flustered, she knocked the glass of milk over. It spilled on Ruth and on the floor. Mom jumped back, her face pale and her hands shaking. Ruth stood up, took two steps, then stopped when her mother backed away.

Carefully, Ruth stressed, "It's all right. The floor is still sticky from all the company yesterday. We don't have to have a clean house, ever."

"I just can't talk about it today. That's all."

Before Ruth could say another word, her mother disappeared out the back door. Ruth followed and watched her mother take off across the street and down toward the park. No doubt Carolyn wished she had a cigarette, but she'd quit the day she'd moved in with Ruth and Megan.

It wasn't the Friday morning Ruth had planned for. Her fingers itched to call Rosa, her best friend, and spill her frustration. Instead, she spent the next two hours enrolling Megan in school and looking for her mother. Just before noon, she dropped Megan off at a friend's. She didn't like it, but the "not knowing" was driving her crazy.

The only good thing about not being able to speak to Rosa was that Sam and Rosa couldn't ask where she was going. Somehow she didn't think they'd approve of her plan.

* * *

A dust cloud announced yet another intruder intent on invading Eric's time and space. That meant the barricades were down. The sheriff, FBI and state police had finally cleared off his land yesterday—a week after he'd discovered the bodies. They'd left yellow tape encircling the shed and strict orders for the area to be left undisturbed.

No one seemed to care enough to look elsewhere. Why should they when a Santellis was involved?

He almost envied the ancestor who'd built this house. Back in ole Sal's day, a shotgun would have clearly indicated No Trespassers. Today, in Eric's day, a shotgun would send him directly back to jail.

A green Jeep loaded with suitcases and an assortment of odd-looking equipment bumped to a stop in front of his porch. At first glance, Eric thought the man behind the wheel had said goodbye to his youth long ago. A closer look indicated that the man had said goodbye to civilization long ago. Everything about him looked old and tired except for his eyes. They were alive and scrutinizing. "Nate McCoy," he said, exiting the Jeep and grabbing a suitcase.

"That should mean something to me?" Eric asked.

"Didn't Sam call?"

"No."

"Call him," Nate suggested.

Since Nate McCoy didn't flash a badge, Eric's first inclination was to order the man off his property, but if Sam was involved, then it was worth a call.

A moment later, Rosa answered, "Packard here."

"Do you know a Nate McCoy? He says he knows Sam and—"

"I'll give you to Sam."

Rosa wasn't being rude, Sam explained after a moment. She was listening to her lawyer's advice about avoiding Broken Bones and Eric until the police had proved something definite. The Rosa Eric had grown up with would have thumbed her nose at authority. The Rosa of today had learned to listen. Eric was learning, too.

Sam took over the conversation. "I tried calling twice, couldn't get through. Nate's a friend of my dad's. He does some kind of government work that he doesn't like to talk about. We've hired him to look over everything and see what he can come up with."

"Crime scene's still cordoned off. I'm supposed to call the sheriff if anyone comes sniffing around."

"It's your call," Sam said. "But I thought you didn't think much of the sheriff."

"I don't think much of anyone," Eric muttered as he put away his cell phone.

Nate McCoy was not a conversationalist. He had Eric take him through each and every step that had occurred since Lucy and Dustin had been discovered. Reenacting the events didn't take that long. Dustin had been buried yesterday. Lucy had been moved days before. Who knew when she'd be buried? Her discovery hadn't warranted the hoopla Dustin's had. Most of the shed's contents had been carted off by the sheriff's department as potential evidence.

Dutifully, Nate wrote down everything Eric said and nodded a dismissal before taking out a cell phone that looked more like a radio. It put Eric's to shame and didn't require the same search for a signal.

Eric retreated to his porch and waited to see what

would happen next. It only took an hour for another dust cloud to appear on the horizon. Doc Winters joined the foray. Once Nate figured out who Doc was and how much knowledge he had of the area, the two men disappeared inside the shed, and Eric returned to his porch with the newspaper Doc tossed him.

"What do you think?" Doc asked a little while later. Eric had been so involved in Ricky's latest article, he hadn't heard the retired doctor walk to the porch.

"About the paper or about Nate?"

"Both."

"Well, I think Nate's closemouthed but I'm glad he's here helping Rosa. As for the paper, I think Ricky's dwelling too much on Rosa's connection to Lucy."

"The sheriff's determined to put that girl away. It's no wonder she's back in the news." Doc settled, uninvited, into a chair. "There are too many people sticking their nose in where they don't belong."

"Like you?" Eric asked.

"Yes, like me. 'Bout time for some adventure." Doc laughed.

Just as Eric was settling in to see what else Ricky had to share, another dust cloud appeared. A small silver SUV crowded in next to Doc's Cadillac and Nate's Jeep. Ruth Atkins stepped from the vehicle. She'd shed her mourning attire, unless her black backpack counted, and dressed in jeans and a T-shirt. Her hair was tied back in a long braid. She stared at Eric, Doc and then the shed. Finally, she shook her head as if dismissing them. She climbed over the yellow tape and headed for the shed.

Eric wondered if, like Doc, she was about to become a confidante of Nate McCoy's. Apparently not. She didn't last a minute. She soon stomped to the porch, nodded at Doc and gave Eric a dirty look before plopping on the front step and pulling out a notebook. "He said he has *nothing* to report," she groused.

"Just another day at Hotel Santellis," Eric muttered.

Doc got right to the point. "What are you doing here, Ruthie?"

"I'm here to prove Rosa innocent."

"And find out what happened to Dustin," Eric guessed.

"And find out what happened to my husband," Ruth agreed. "Sam claims he checked your place just after Dustin disappeared. According to the police reports, that shed was checked more than once. It makes no sense. Somehow my husband wound up in your shed. I want to know how and why and when."

"You know, Ruthie, some things are best left alone," Doc gently said.

Setting her notebook aside, and without asking permission, she went inside the cabin. Soon Eric heard the sound of furniture moving.

"It bother you that she's in there?" Doc asked. He scooted the rocking chair around and peered into the cabin.

"I've got nothing to hide."

"But she's going through your personal belongings." Doc looked appalled.

"I don't have any personal belongings. I have two sets of clothes and a toothbrush. The only things I've purchased for the cabin, besides tools, are a lamp, a bed and a couch. Everything else was already here if I haven't carted it off as trash. If she finds something, I'll be the first to shout hallelujah."

Doc seemed content to stay on the porch and watch Nate. Eric wanted to watch Ruth, but he doubted she'd welcome his company. He opted for some outside activity. Nothing worked up a sweat more than throwing trash in the bed of an old Ford pickup. Two hours later, Ruth exited the cabin. Her red hair was dusted with dirt, the knees of her pants were brown and both cheeks looked as if she'd cried tears of mud. She marched past Eric and Doc and went straight for the shed, only to return before the two men could even begin to discuss how long it would take Nate to boot her.

"This time McCoy says he has nothing *definite* to report," she grumbled. Short of stature, short on words and short on time, the retired crime-scene investigator seemed determined to keep everyone but Doc out. Ruth picked up her notebook again and stared at the shed thoughtfully. Eric could almost believe she was planning a break-in.

"Maybe he hasn't found anything yet," Eric said. "Did you find anything?"

"You have mice."

"I meant," Eric said slowly. "Did you find anything interesting?"

"I find mice to be interesting." With that, she closed the notebook she'd been writing in, walked to the SUV and left without saying goodbye.

"That woman's driven," Eric said.

"Maybe a bit too much," Doc agreed.

The next morning, Eric wondered if Doc might be right. Nate arrived at seven, Doc at eight and Ruth showed up just after ten. She managed to get Nate to utter a few sentences, something neither Doc nor Eric had been able to do.

When Ruth finally left Nate and settled on the porch steps, she glanced at her watch. "I dropped Megan off at a birthday party at eight. I've got to be there at about five. They're doing a picnic at the park and such." She shook her head and looked at Doc. "Usually, I'd stay and help, but I wanted to be here. I hope Megan understands."

Her face softened when she said Megan's name. It was a look Eric hadn't noticed before, one he could learn to enjoy.

For the next few hours, like little old men gathered on the benches in front of a barbershop, Eric, Doc and Ruth watched Nate's unorthodox methods. Eric and Doc with a sort of edge-of-the-seat anticipation, as if a tennis match were right in front of them, and Ruth with a court stenographer's dedication. She documented every crazy thing Nate did, like repeatedly measuring the width of the door and carrying a fake body in and out of the shed. Sometimes the fake body's head was dragging. Sometimes the fake body's head hit the top of the door. Sometimes Nate dropped the fake body. Then, Nate added weight to the fake body and finally invited his audience to play. He had first Doc, then Eric and finally Ruth carry the fake body in and out of the shed. He then measured their heights and put white chalk marks on the door frames. Doc was the tallest, followed by Eric, then Nate and finally Ruth. It was the first time he invited them to share in the investigation. It inspired Ruth to make a phone call and then hang around a little longer.

Good thing, too, because a news crew showed up at dusk. The press camped out at the end of the driveway, still on the road, and not violating the No Trespassing signs. They ventured closer than Eric liked and managed to take more than one picture before Ruth and a good deal of police jargon concerning privacy and ongoing investigation rights finally chased them away. Ruth seemed almost energized after the encounter. She finished off the first notebook and started on a second.

And Eric watched her every move and forgot that he was hungry. He tried not to let it bother him that he was starting to enjoy the company of a woman who considered his family guilty of murdering her husband; he tried not to let it bother him that she, as a police officer, probably knew more about their criminal activity than he did; he tried not to let it bother him that she represented what he wanted most in life: someone who truly knew how to love.

He'd spent most of his adult years trying to avoid his family; she'd spent the last few years of her adult life chasing his family.

Neither of them had been successful.

NINE

Sunday morning Megan skipped across the parking lot and disappeared inside the church while Ruth stood frozen by her SUV. She should have used a different church to bury Dustin. This church housed friends, neighbors and hope for the future. But, if she couldn't make her legs move so she could go inside, what was inside was useless.

Of course, the motivation to move had just closed the door behind her without a "Bye, Mom" or even a wave. Ruth had never allowed her five-year-old to traverse the parking lot alone. A few churchgoers waved and looked concerned. She nodded that she was okay and hoped no one came her way. Her feet still refused to move, even after the front parking lot filled and people starting pulling around to the back. Taking a deep breath, Ruth checked the church's front door. It was open. The greeters, a couple who lived just a block from Ruth, shook hands, handed little carnations to the visitors and gently herded the masses in. Had Megan made it to class? To the kindergarten class? Big Girl Class, Megan called it.

Megan would also be on her own tomorrow, the first day of kindergarten. Big girl school.

Too many changes.

And she felt so alone facing them.

Twenty minutes later, Ruth finally made it to class. It was full, and she had to take a seat up front. Not her favorite place, but then, today was definitely not her favorite day. She wanted to be at Eric's making sure she didn't miss anything. But, she needed to be here, in Gila City, staying close to her daughter and meeting with God.

An hour and twenty minutes later, Ruth watched as Megan buckled herself in the child seat in the back and picked up her coloring book. Ruth stood immobile by the door of her SUV and waited for Sam and Rosa to approach. They'd completely missed Sunday school and had been late to the main service. Considering the pale look on Rosa's face, Ruth figured both pregnancy and the police scrutiny were proving upsetting. No surprise there.

"I have a few questions," Ruth said.

Rosa paled a bit more, and Ruth almost felt guilty. The gag order was proving more difficult than they'd imagined. For two friends who'd spoken on the phone to each other every day, barely speaking just didn't work.

"I just have a couple, nothing that will compromise the investigation, I promise."

Rosa glanced at Sam and then nodded. Even though she was the color of milk, Rosa looked radiant. Ruth wanted to tell her it would soon be better but she was afraid to say the words for fear they wouldn't come true.

Sometimes things didn't get better.

"How come I didn't know about Nate McCoy?" Ruth asked.

"That we hired him to nose around Eric's place or that he existed?" Sam leaned against Ruth's SUV and dragged

Rosa with him. The arm he casually looped around his wife looked both relaxed and protective, yet he looked weary.

Sam knew her too well. Anyone else would have simply mentioned the nosing around Eric's place.

"Both," Ruth said.

"It's actually more Dad's doing than mine. Nate's the son of one of his old war buddies," Sam said. "Nate, lucky for us, not so lucky for the government, is taking leave right now. He was some sort of forensic specialist for the government, probably a whole lot more than that judging by what I've seen him do. Dad's calling his working for us therapy. I, personally, don't care what you call it. So far, Nate's a big help. Mallery messed up—"

"We're not supposed to share all this," Rosa whispered. She was looking at Ruth and not at her husband. Her hand dropped to her stomach and suddenly it was all too clear to Ruth just how much she was asking.

Ruth felt her teeth grind together. She closed her eyes. Finally, she managed, "He barely answers my questions. Even if they have nothing to do with you. Why?"

"Mommy," Megan called from the backseat. "I finished my coloring page. Can we go now?"

"Just a minute, Megan." Ruth turned back to Sam. "Work with me. Throw me a bone. Something. Anything."

"I told him you were okay. That he could trust you." Sam shot Rosa a look. Ruth recognized it. It was the typical look a husband gave his wife when he wanted her to let him do all the talking. Rosa had every right to be concerned. She knew how skewed justice could be. Ruth had learned the same lesson many times. But this time, justice would prevail. She'd make sure of it.

"Telling him I'm okay and that he can trust me didn't work. He hasn't told me anything. *Anything.*"

Megan started chanting, "Wanna go home. Wanna go home," and leaned forward. The last few straggling families heading to their cars, paused, checked to see if everything was all right and continued on.

"I know," Sam said softly. "I tried telling Nate that he could trust you. It's just Nate knows firsthand how not to trust. He, well, let's just say he had a case go sour because of a slip of the tongue."

"So," Ruth said slowly, "Nate won't talk to me because he's been burned. You won't talk to me because your lawyer has said not to. Sam, tell me, who will talk to me?" It amazed her that she even had to ask. This man had been her partner on the force. They'd shared everything: job, meals, heartbreak.

"I can't—" Sam started

"We can't," Rosa finished. "They found Lucy's purse in the shed, with my prints on it. Nate believes whoever carried Dustin's body into the shed was tall, about my height. Both Lucy and Dustin were probably killed with the exact make of gun I carry."

It was the something, the anything, Ruth wanted. She'd read Dustin's autopsy report carefully; it hadn't mentioned the type of gun. Matter of fact, the gun part was hazy.

"Ruthie," Sam said, "the lawyer specifically said not to risk compromising the investigation because of our close association to you."

"But, I'm on your side. I believe Rosa's innocent."

"But you didn't believe, not at first," Rosa said softly. "When that deputy suggested they could tie me to the crime, you stepped back. Away from me. I remember."

Unfortunately, Ruth remembered, too. And if Sam and Rosa's lawyer had made such a big deal out of Ruth's obvious disbelief, then someday a prosecutor might bring up the same concern. Ruth knew where it would happen. In a courtroom. With a slip of the tongue, Nate McCoy had destroyed a stranger's life. With the slip of the foot, Ruth might have done the same thing.

Only Rosa was no stranger, she was a friend.

For a man who'd desperately wanted to be left alone, being alone felt pretty lonely. Sunday morning dragged.

Eric figured Doc and his wife had headed into town and the big white church on the corner. Doc would probably spend the afternoon being coddled by that wife of his and catching up on all the catnaps he claimed to miss. Nate didn't look or act like a churchgoing guy. Eric figured he was in a lab somewhere breaking down dirt samples for traces of blood. It wasn't hard to imagine what Ruth was doing with her day. Probably spending it with her daughter, doing mommy things like putting together puzzles or playing hopscotch or finger painting.

That's what his mom had done with his sister.

Sweat trickled down Eric's forehead. Arizona in late August still resembled an oven left on for too long. Not that the weather inspired him to go inside. Most of his time at Florence Penitentiary had been spent outdoors in the heat.

Doc suffered the most from the unrelenting sun, but claimed he'd never had so much fun. Nate, well, Nate didn't talk enough to know if he was as blasé as he appeared. Ruth did the best, but she was driven. They were all probably enjoying their Biblical day of rest holed up in air-conditioned rooms. And now, come to think of it, would be a good time for Eric, the good son, to spend some time in an air-conditioned room. His father's.

It wasn't lost on Eric the irony that *he* was the son his father least respected. How it would anger old Yano Santellis to know that during the last days of his life, it was Eric who gave Yano the most respect.

Truthfully, the respect was a thorn in Eric's side. He wanted nothing to do with his father. He blamed his father, not the system, for the wasted years in prison. The only thing Eric wanted to do after his release was find Mary—it sounded as though she'd had just as tough a time as he'd had—make sure she was all right and then disappear.

After a month of looking for Mary in Italy, he'd moved his search back to Arizona, and having no luck, he'd decided to visit his father and see if that helped.

It hadn't. Eric's first visit to his father, just over two months ago, had been a rude awakening. Yano lived in a small room, painted pond-scum green, which had a window that offered a view of the building next door.

Eric wouldn't have recognized the man standing in the middle of the room had he passed him on the street or even been seated next to him. Yano was taking clothes out of the closet and putting them in piles on the floor. He'd also taken whatever he was wearing off, and they were probably on the floor along with the bedding and the curtains that should block the view to the building next door. The hospital bed wasn't made; it didn't even have bedding. All the drawers of the dresser were open and empty. A jar with false teeth sat on the table next to the bed.

Yano had turned when he heard Eric clear his throat and said, "They're stealing my money."

"What money?"

Yano gave Eric a dirty look. No surprise. But his next words were: "Who are you?"

"Ahem." A nurse stood in the doorway. She didn't look happy. "You could be the King of England, and he wouldn't know you, *and* he'd still accuse you of taking his money—as if he had any. He never has visitors except for cops and reporters and even they've given up now."

Two weeks later he had his dad out of that Alzheimer's unit. Assisted living at a private retirement home cost more, and the private nurses cost even more than that. And the new staff knew that Yano had a faithful visitor and to screen out cops and the media. Not that his dad was even aware Eric visited. Like today.

Eric drove into Phoenix at noon. He parked in a well-maintained parking lot, entered a foyer alive with art and plant life and then signed the guest book before taking an elevator to the second floor. Today Yano was dressed. He wore gray sweatpants and a plaid shirt. His feet were bare, a sight Eric couldn't recall from his childhood. But, then, his father hadn't spent much time at home. When Eric entered, Yano stood and went to look out the window. His view, now, was of desert landscaping. Yano pressed a hand against the glass and asked, "Do you have a dollar?"

Eric pulled out his wallet and handed his father a dollar. "What do you need it for?"

"Cab fare." Yano stayed at the window, studying the activities outside, and looking pensive.

After a minute, when it didn't appear Yano was in the mood for small talk, Eric said. "Are you going somewhere?"

"Haven't made up my mind."

Eric nodded. "I'm going somewhere. I've moved into the cabin up in Broken Bones."

"Does Eric know?"

Eric didn't even blink. "Yeah, I think so." Never, not on a single Sunday, had Yano realized which son was visiting. Most of the time he thought Eric was Tony. Oh, the orders Yano gave, the places a young Tony had gone— places unfit for men with scruples, but not unfit for Yano Santellis's son. Sometimes Yano thought Eric was Sardi. And always Sardi was instructed to listen, if not to Yano, then to Tony. Once, Yano had called Eric, "Father." On that day, Yano had curled up on his bed in a fetal position.

Yano shook his head. "Eric's a strange kid. If he didn't look so much like his grandfather, I'd be mad at your mother."

"I didn't realize there was a resemblance."

"I think that's why Eric got the cabin. You should see the pictures. I've got them here somewhere."

Eric doubted that. When they'd moved Yano to Orange Grove Estates, Yano packed three suitcases.

Yano turned from the window and sat on the bed's edge. The bare feet made him look vulnerable. Old and young at the same time. "Tony," Yano said, looking straight at Eric, "while you're up in Broken Bones, maybe you should do something about Eddie? He's taking too many chances."

"What kind of chances?"

"He's taking too many cars from his own backyard. Tell Eddie I'll take the car lot away from him."

Eric started. Just how long ago had Yano had this conversation with Tony.

"I'll talk to Eddie, Father."

"You do that. Oh, and tell Mallery I want to see him."

TEN

It was dark when Eric finally drove up the driveway to the cabin. He'd forgotten to leave a light on. After parking, he left the headlights on and went into the cabin. A few minutes later, Eric exited with a lantern in his hand. Determination was a tangible entity. A Mallery was in charge of finding who'd put the bodies in his shed. If the Mallerys were friends with his father, a Mallery might have put the bodies in his shed. Even a Mallery who went by the title of sheriff.

Rosa didn't stand a chance.

Eric decided to ignore Nate's order to leave the shed alone. After all, it was Eric's shed, smell and all. Of course, it didn't look at all like the shed Eric had discovered the body in. Almost every item had been bagged and taken somewhere for scrutiny. Now that Nate was on the scene, a string and four sticks had taken up residence in corners where a body had not been discovered. In white chalk, Nate had also written some sort of shorthand on the shed's wall. White chalk marked the doorway. Apparently where one of the bodies had connected with the door. Exploring the almost-empty shed took all of five minutes and was so unrewarding, Eric didn't even get the satisfaction of feeling he'd righteously trespassed or pushed the limits.

Hah! He wasn't in jail, *this was his home* and he no longer needed to worry about limits. He was a free man—a free man who wished he'd honored Nate's request and had left the shed alone.

Eric didn't know if his discomfort came from too long a time spent in jail and learning the consequences of rule breaking or if the discomfort came from disregarding a request coming from a man he actually respected.

One whose sole purpose was helping Rosa.

It was Megan's first day of kindergarten. Ruth followed a line of cars into a small parking lot already too crowded with the vehicles of staff combined with the vehicles of anxious kindergarten parents. The street parking rivaled the lot parking. Ruth finally found a spot half a block away.

Megan was more than ready, which she proved by not waiting for Ruth's help. With the click of a seat belt and a gymnastic move not recommended for children under five, Megan was out of her booster seat in a matter of moments—before Ruth could even get out of the car. Talk about not feeling needed. Megan had even dressed herself this morning. A pink shirt with sparkly sequins topped a pair of slightly bell-bottom pink pants. Pink sandals that clomped when Megan walked and showed pink-painted toenails—Ruth's mother's influence—clad Megan's feet. Two handmade bead necklaces, one pink and made by Megan and the other white and made by Mommy, dangled from Megan's neck.

Ruth was sure the teacher would faint right away when Megan the fashion plate walked into the classroom.

"Mrs. Atkins. Wait." The woman approaching Ruth had dark hair and dragged a little boy behind her. He, in turn, dragged a good-sized plush superhero doll behind him.

Maybe pink wasn't so bad.

Now this is what Ruth expected—to have a child who didn't want to leave her mommy to go to school, but no, instead she had a little girl ready to embrace the world.

Thank goodness Megan was more like Dustin than Ruth.

"Almando, stop fighting me. Look, here's Megan from your Sunday-school class. Show her how brave you are."

"Tia Santos," Ruth said. "How are you doing?"

Tia smiled. It didn't quite reach her eyes, but then it hadn't even been two weeks since her father-in-law Jose's funeral. "We're doing okay. You know Manny."

Megan stared at Manny with disdain.

"Megan, say hello," Ruth urged. "It's Manny from your Bible school. Won't it be nice to have a friend in class?"

"Heeellllooooo," Megan said slowly as ordered. She didn't answer the question and Ruth didn't press. With a five-year-old, tone was everything, and Ruth could tell the answer about having Manny in class would be a resounding No.

Tia pushed Manny closer to Megan. Out of the side of her mouth, she said, "Grandpa Jose always took the kids to school. That's how all his brothers arrived. Manny's convinced being dropped off by a mommy instead of a grandpa is some kind of kindergarten embarrassment."

And just like that, Ruth felt as though her legs had been cut off beneath her knees. This morning had been so hectic: packing Megan's lunch, gathering Megan's school things and trying to convince both Megan and Grandma that Megan's attire was all wrong. She'd been so focused on Megan and herself that she forgot the other person missing from their morning, from their lives.

There were only a few fathers walking with their small children into the school building. Mommies outnumbered daddies about ten to one.

Manny suffered because he didn't have a grandfather to add to the mix. Megan didn't even know enough to be sad that her daddy was missing. But she did know it was time to hurry. Just the way Megan had disappeared into the church yesterday, now she was disappearing into the school building. She knew where to go. They'd come last week and met the teacher, toured the school, gotten the supply list. Still, there were hundreds of kids, pushing, running, yelling. Megan might get frightened!

The way Ruth was frightened.

Pushing open the school doors, she hurried away from Tia, away from facing the truth, her fear.

Megan stood in front of the hallway coatracks.

"Mommy, where do I hang my lunch box?"

Together they found the hook with Megan's name, written on a green frog, above it. Then, Ruth followed Megan into the classroom. Megan's desk was the first one in row one. Manny Santos was the fifth desk in row four. Tia knelt by her son emptying pencils and folders and such into his desk. Megan did that without asking Ruth for help. Ruth took the tissues and other items brought to share with the class to the teacher's desk.

It only took Miss Forest five minutes to give Megan the nickname of Pinkerbell—which pleased Megan to no end—and to clear the room of parents. She was a professional. Ruth took two steps down the school's hallway, then turned to peek in the window. Two mothers, looking a lot like twins, blocked the doorway and stared into the room. It would take a crowbar to move them.

Tia again touched Ruth's arm. "You want to go out for coffee and talk?"

"No, I have something to do." Every day, for the next six weeks, after Ruth dropped Megan off, she planned to investigate Dustin's death. She hadn't had the knowledge, the contacts, or the means three years ago. Today she had that, and the time off from work. She headed for the door and freedom.

"Some other time then?" Tia asked.

Ruth pushed open the door and stepped into the sunshine. "I'll think about it."

"Good." Tia seemed willing to assume the *maybe* to mean *yes.*

As they walked to their cars, Ruth started to reword her "I'll think about it" into a stronger form of *maybe,* but two police cars went past them and turned into the school parking lot.

The sight was enough to silence both women.

"One of the kids…"

"No, the sirens aren't on."

Ruth hurried back to the parking lot and skidded to a stop at the trunk of the second patrol car. Tia was right behind her. The two mothers who looked like twins were standing in the middle of an empty parking place. One was crying; the other looked angry.

"I parked it right here," said the crying one.

"We were only inside about thirty minutes," said the angry one. "Surely you'll find a witness or something. It's a busy parking lot."

"You'll get my car back, won't you?" finished the crying one.

Ruth knew both officers. One nodded at her, but it was business and the number of cars stolen in Gila City had been skyrocketing for too many years. The mayor had promised the civilians action and the police were under orders to get it done *now.* Ruth let them do their jobs.

"Not another one," Tia moaned.

"In broad daylight," Ruth agreed.

"They're getting bolder." Tia dragged her feet, silent for a moment, before finally saying, "Do you suppose it was a kid?"

Ruth wanted to answer, wanted to assure Tia that fifteen-year-olds, like the one who killed her father-in-law, were few and far between, but it would be a lie.

Luckily, Ruth was saved from having to say much. They'd reached their cars. "I don't know, but they'll catch whoever did it."

Tia nodded. "Yeah."

"I need to get going. Thanks for the invite to coffee. If—"

Tia interrupted, "No ifs. We'll do it some morning."

Sliding behind the wheel of her car, Ruth could only nod. Coffee with a potential friend? If only she could.

Careful not to hit the cars of any other numb kindergarten parents, Ruth pulled into traffic and checked her watch. Straight up nine. She'd get to Broken Bones and Eric's place about ten, and she'd stay until two. Four hours a day she'd give to finding Dustin's killer.

Doc arrived first on Monday morning in shorts and a T-shirt and looked both ridiculous and uncomfortable.

"Wife suggested it," he admitted. Eric figured Mrs. Doc must be one smart lady.

Nate arrived a minute later, unloaded some equipment from the back of his Jeep, scanned the porch as if looking for something, or someone, and then went right to the shed. "Guess he didn't need either of us," Doc groused.

Eric figured Doc "needed" to feel needed. Retired, and living in the middle of nowhere, probably meant lots of hours to fill. Why not fill them just down the road where something unusual was happening?

So for the next few hours, Doc spent his time keeping track of Nate and solving crossword puzzles while Eric ascertained his roof didn't leak, assessed his windows and washed the ones that didn't need replacing.

Ruth finally arrived about ten o'clock. Once again she'd donned jeans and a T-shirt. Settling down on the front step, she found her perfect spot, opened her backpack and took out her notebook. She studied the layout. "What did I miss yesterday?"

"Nothing. No one showed up. Where were you?" It had surprised him, how at odds he'd felt yesterday without Nate, Doc and Ruth to watch. It also surprised him how tempted he was to share what his father had said about Mallery. But, no, he was part of this little committee by circumstance, not by invitation. Plus, the people he had included in his life had a strange way of dying. He'd pursue the Mallery angle on his own, just as soon as he heard what Nate had to offer.

"Sunday commitments," Doc said.

"Church," Ruth agreed.

"Were Rosa and Sam at church?" Eric asked. The way he figured, the only thing missing from their little party was Rosa and Sam.

"Of course they were there. They never miss." Ruth didn't look at him when she answered. "Megan started school today, and so we spent most of yesterday filling her supply list."

"I remember when schools supplied everything," Doc said.

"I'm just grateful they supplied everything when I went to school. No way would my dad have put out money for scissors and tissues and stuff." Ruth said it so matter-of-factly that Eric almost missed just how close to the surface her emotions were. He knew little or nothing about her life before Dustin disappeared. He was as guilty of assumptions as anyone.

"You're handling this well," Doc said. "Need anything?"

"I need to find out what happened to Dustin." Ruth started drawing, effectively shutting Eric and Doc out. Her notebook probably had ten variations on the shed. It was obvious that Van Gogh had nothing to worry about. All of Ruth's sheds looked like shoes. Doc stood, took a moment to study what Ruth was doing, and then shook his head. Eric didn't have to ask why. This time, Ruth's shoe also had what looked to be fish where the windows should be.

"This is better than television," Doc said ruefully. Then added, "Wife says you both need to come down to the house for lunch, get a real meal in those bellies of yours and get away from this."

"Your wife's nuts." Eric responded since it looked as if Ruth couldn't tear herself away from her drawing.

"She is, and she'll pick your brain for some new book on Broken Bones she's busy writing."

"She's a writer?"

"She calls herself more of an historian. She wrote a history of Broken Bones almost thirty years ago and had it self-published. She's made enough off the sale of that book to buy us a Hummer."

"Why'd you want a Hummer?"

"I didn't. She did."

Eric grinned. Mrs. Doc just might be worth knowing.

Nate exited the shed, put on gloves, and with a flashlight and good old get-down-on-your-knees-and-get-digging-determination, started moving some dirt near the side of the shed. He picked something off the ground and put it in a plastic bag. Then, he fetched a shovel from his Jeep and went back in the shed.

The moment of light banter disappeared. Ruth stood up and ventured down the path to get a closer look. She and Nate exchanged a few words. Nate shook his head. Ruth stormed back. "This nothing-definite-to-report business is getting old."

"Dustin's body leaned against that wall," Doc remarked. "He's looking for traces of tissue."

"Why would tissue be evident on the wall since the consensus is he died somewhere else?" Eric asked.

"I think Nate's trying to figure out how long Dustin was in the shed before you found him," Ruth said.

"Can they do that?" Eric asked.

"They can do just about anything nowadays." Ruth didn't have time to say more because Nate came out of the shed and handed her his cell phone. Frowning, she took it and said, "Hello." The conversation was mostly one-sided and not on Ruth's. Emotion danced across her face: anger, remorse, understanding and agreement. "We'll do that," she finally said.

Handing Nate his phone back, she made a face at him before standing, and then looked at the two men sitting in their rocking chairs and for once staring intently at her instead of staring intently at whatever Nate was doing.

"Sam wants us to take off for a while. Seems Nate called him. We're distracting him."

"Sam is telling me to take off," Eric said slowly, "of my own land."

"For Rosa." The way she said it told Eric that the *for Rosa* had been the trump card used to convince Ruth, too.

ELEVEN

"There's a café in town," Ruth said.

"You want to go there?" Surprised, Eric studied the woman in front of him. She almost looked approachable. Was a little bit of healing happening, maybe?

Matter-of-factly, Ruth continued, "It's the town hang-out. Maybe we'll hear something. The locals have been curious. We've been so intent on keeping track of Nate, we've sorta forgotten there were others involved."

"I don't think there were others involved," Doc said.

"Sometimes," Ruth asserted, "it's not the obvious that solves the crime, but the not so obvious." She looked at the shed.

Eric agreed. Between the local authorities, the CSI techs and now Nate, any secrets the shed contained should be exposed. As a matter of fact, any secrets outside the shed should be exposed, too. Eric had watched all morning as Nate checked tire treads. If Eric been allowed to finish his schooling, maybe he'd be the one checking for tire treads. Unwilling to let himself dwell on the past, Eric headed inside to retrieve his wallet from beside the bed.

"You realize," he said to Ruth when he returned, "that going to the café with me will cause more talk about what we're doing together than what happened to Dustin."

"I'm counting on that. Surprise will loosen tongues."

"Not a bad idea," Eric agreed.

Doc shook his head, made a cell-phone call to his wife and then as he meandered to his car, grumbled about the café's chicken-fried steak and the cost.

Ruth and Eric watched him for a moment before heading for their own vehicles. The Last Chance Café wasn't quite a run to town. It was more on the outskirts. John Billings, who was also the mayor of Gila City, probably hoped to lure some of the highway crowd. Too bad the road to Broken Bones epitomized lonely. Still, judging by the crowd, Ruth was right. The locals used the café as a meeting place. Before he made it to the entrance, the hum of conversation reminded Eric of bees, lots of bees. The moment he opened the door and stepped in, the bees flew out the window.

Silence reigned, and Ruth motioned. "We're right here." Heads turned to watch him walk across the room. No one said a word.

When he made it to the booth, Eric paused before sitting, and announced, "Yes, I'm Eric Santellis. Yes, I do eat lunch. And, yes, it's somewhat amazing to see me eating with Mrs. Dustin Atkins. Keep in mind, she's trying to find a killer. I'm not him."

"Well," said Doc, before Eric could sit down, but not before a handful of people left, "that was subtle."

"It worked. They're all talking about us." He looked at Ruth. "Start eavesdropping."

She bit her bottom lip and shook her head. "Look at the counter."

Ricky the reporter grinned and waved. Then, he stood and came over. "Hi, Ruthie."

He sat next to Doc, leaving the spot next to Ruth for Eric. The good folks of Broken Bones would not only witness Eric and Ruth sharing a meal, but also sharing a bench.

She scooted over and handed him a menu.

"Ricky," Doc said. "I don't think you're welcome here. We've got business to discuss."

"Hey," protested Ricky. "I've been fair in my coverage. More than you got from the state and national press. Keep me informed, and I won't disappoint."

"Hmm," Eric mused, "a newspaperman who claims integrity."

"I read the newspaper stories," Ruth said. "Ricky, good job."

Ricky pulled a small notebook out of his pocket. "Knew I should have brought my laptop, but every time I bring it out in this restaurant, everyone stops talking."

"Smart crowd," Eric commented.

"So," Ricky said, looking at Ruth, "I take it by the camaraderie that you're convinced Eric had nothing to do with Dustin's murder?"

Eric looked at Ruth. He'd not had the guts to ask her point-blank. She paused a moment, but finally, she nodded. "Eric had nothing to do with Dustin's disappearance."

"So," Ricky asked, "what brings you here? I'd think you'd be sticking close to Eric's cabin, making sure nothing goes wrong."

"Off the record, we got kicked out," Ruth said. "Nate needed some time alone."

"Nate McCoy." Ricky nodded. "I spent Saturday night researching him. Did you know he was personally requested by the last president to investigate the murder of a White House staff member?"

"You're saying," Doc said slowly, "that Nate McCoy actually knows the president."

"And not just ours. I found references linking him to Zambia's president and Iceland's president. He's really been around."

"Guess I need to trust him," Ruth muttered.

Doc looked a bit shell-shocked. "I've always wanted to meet a president. Guess I need to believe you about him being able to tell by tissue residue how long the bodies were in your shed. I'm just amazed how far medicine has come. I've only been retired for ten years."

"The autopsy report wound up being twenty-two pages," Ruth said. "They know the time of day, his position in the car when he was shot…." Her words drifted off as she summed up her husband's last moments. "He was shot in the head and died instantly. He was carried to the shed, much later, in a body bag."

Ricky finally started writing in his notebook. Of course, that last bit had only become common knowledge recently. No wonder he was intrigued. "Makes you wonder what kind of murderers have access to body bags?"

Eric started. That hadn't even crossed his mind. Maybe reporters were good for something. Ricky continued, "And Lucille Straus's autopsy report was thirty-six pages long." Ricky said reverently, "Turns out she died approximately two months ago. First somebody thunked her on the head and then they shot her."

"Are you ready to order?" The waitress stepped up to the table. She looked at Eric. Since he'd grown up with thunking and shooting conversation being bantered around the supper table, he didn't mind ordering first.

"I was sitting over there," Ricky said. He obviously had a strong stomach, too. "My hamburger should be about done."

"I'll have a hamburger, too." Ruth set aside the menu she hadn't bothered to open.

"Chicken-fried steak," said Doc. Then he looked at his boothmates and ordered, "Don't tell Elizabeth.

"Excuse me." Doc nudged Ricky right after the waitress hurried away. A moment later, the old man headed toward a hallway marked Restroom.

"I think all this talk about violence is bothering him. He's getting tense." Ricky sat back down.

"He should retire somewhere," Eric said. "Live a life of ease."

"Elizabeth would never go for that. Her family's been here forever," Ricky said. "Plus, they might not have the money."

"They always had money," Ruth said.

"Not after he was sued. That's when his wife starting pinching pennies."

Ruth shook her head. "The Bible has it right. It says somewhere not to sue your brother. I know an officer who took a bullet rather than shoot an offender. He was afraid of being sued."

"I took one of my final criminal-justice classes while I was in prison," Eric added, "The textbook said that more cops fear being sued than being murdered."

"It's nuts," Ruth agreed. "Doc and Elizabeth gave so

much to the community. I never heard they'd been sued.
I'm surprised."

"About five years ago." Ricky closed his notebook.
"Most people were appalled. It was an out-of-state couple.
She went into labor early and Doc happened upon them
and literally delivered a baby girl on the side of the road.
Baby wound up with some type of brain damage. Doc's
insurance covered most of it, but he'd never made that
much practicing in Broken Bones. Half the time, he prac-
ticed for free. The lawsuit wound up using their savings
and, since Doc's retired, not as much is coming in. Good
thing the couple doesn't live here. They'd be tarred and
feathered."

Ruth's eyes dropped. Women hated hearing sad stories
about babies. Eric looked around the restaurant so he
wouldn't have to see the sorrowful expression on her face.
Most of the occupants still cast guarded looks in his direction. Of course, they weren't looking that fondly at
Ruth, either. He wondered if she cared. Then, she patted
him on the hand. It surprised him, the act of kindness.
And, he wished that instead of patting his hand, she'd held
his hand. It was a ridiculous wish.

Somewhat embarrassed, he studied the decor of the
café. Rustic was the best word to describe it. The floor was
sprinkled with sawdust. All sorts of old-time paraphernalia, such as old guns, bullet molds, rusty horseshoes,
faded newspaper articles and black-and-white photos,
were squished between shaggy animal heads.

One caught his eye. "Isn't that Doc?" Eric pointed to
a black-and-white photo next to their booth.

"His wife, Elizabeth, is next to him." Ruth leaned
closer to get a good look. "Wow, they were young."

"Aging happens to the best of us." Doc waited for Ricky to let him back into his seat. Then, he looked at the photo. "That was taken in 1942 at a carnival. Elizabeth took a prize in sharpshooting. She was the only female to compete."

Ricky's notebook reappeared.

Doc grinned and watched as Ricky wrote down the information. "Young man, go ahead and add I was in the competition, too. She beat me."

Their food arrived. Between passing the ketchup, getting extra napkins and spilling gravy on the table, the topic turned to guns: who owned them and what kind. Ricky not only absorbed every tidbit they threw him, he had a few of his own. Lucille Straus's autopsy had generated some interesting speculation. As stated, it appeared she'd been clubbed before being shot. Then, came the debate between two coroners. The first coroner said both Lucy and Dustin had been shot with the same gun, based on the bullet's circumvention. Coroner number two, called in because coroner number one thought the bullet holes looked a bit odd, said two different guns. Similar, but different. No actual bullets had been recovered, which caused the coroner grief. Lucy had an exit wound. Dustin didn't.

The debate was driving the CSI techs nuts. They knew the probable size of the gun, but unfortunately, not the make. They knew it had to have been a small gun, but with a kick. Both Lucy and Dustin died from a gunshot to the head—which was why Rosa went from a woman who knew Lucy, to a woman who could be highly suspected in Lucy's death. Rosa owned a Beretta 21, a small gun with a kick, and the police knew it. Rosa also had been a nurse before becoming a cop. She'd know how to remove a bullet.

What was most interesting was that Dustin had died instantly and been moved to the shed years later. Lucy hadn't died instantly; she'd died in the shed.

On Tuesday morning, Doc brought the Phoenix paper with him. Although Ricky's name was mentioned as a contributing reporter, this front-page story was written by a seasoned professional and Dustin Atkins received top billing. This journalist milked the dead-cop angle— Arizona's finest, fatherless child, grieving widow becomes cop in her quest for justice.

And it didn't hurt that Ruth Atkins photographed well.

Ruth might have chased them away Saturday but she obviously hadn't acted quickly enough. The press caught her on Eric's front porch. She'd been talking *with* him but looking *past* him. The photographer caught the essence of a determined woman who clearly wanted to be anywhere but where she was. She no longer resembled the lost soul who'd sat in his living room with her head bowed. The photo showed a woman who stood tall, had her chin up, and whose dark gaze clearly accused Eric of not telling her enough.

Eric wished he could remember what the conversation had been about. He knew it had taken place Saturday because she wore the black jeans and red T-shirt that made her look too young to be a mother, a widow and a cop. The outfit also made him wish his last name was anything but Santellis. The photographer caught Ruth standing dangerously close to Eric, and she'd been the one intent on intimidation—all five foot four of her!

Next, Eric picked up the *Gila City Gazette*. Looked as though Ricky had made a tough deadline last night. His story took the Santellis-Atkins dilemma a step further. Besides mentioning the crime scene and all it entailed, he also spent time on Broken Bones history. He wrote about the Riddell Mine and about the Chinese tunnels. He wrote about Ruth's father's shady past, and he wrote about Doc's retirement and his wife's sharpshooting abilities, as well as her book.

Ricky didn't mention the make of Rosa's gun or the missing bullets. Maybe Eric could grow to like the guy. Putting the paper down, he checked out Ruth's whereabouts. She was, once again, returning from the shed. Only, this time she looked happy.

He wondered if she'd seen the *Gila City Gazette* and the reference to her father.

"Nate wants to know if you have any shovels."

"Why?"

"He needs help digging."

Doc turned a little pale. "Digging? What will we be digging?"

Ruth hadn't stuck around to answer, and Eric figured his answer was the same one that had already turned Doc's face pale.

The police had carted off the good shovel, but a quick search turned up another one. The splintered handle didn't stop Ruth. She'd taken it from Eric's hand and was halfway to the shed before he realized she intended to dig with or without him. He caught up, followed by Doc, who moved pretty good for an older man.

The shovel Nate had fetched on Monday had been put

to good use. The sticks and rope were gone, replaced by a decent-size hole. Without pausing, Ruth squatted down and jumped in to assist.

Eric stood above, taking in the scene, and what definitely looked like a grave.

TWELVE

"It's a root cellar," Doc said, sounding both surprised and relieved.

Ruth was knee-deep in the hole. Sweat, dirt and fatigue made her, for some reason, look impressive, beautiful, someone Eric could admire. She carefully stepped away from the opening under her shovel. Without taking her eyes off the faint outline of gravel steps leading down into darkness, she asked, "What's a root cellar?"

"It's a place to store vegetables," Nate said.

"I'll bet this one was dug for a different purpose." Doc peered down. "Like a place to hide from Indians."

"Well, let's see what's down there." Eric picked up Ruth's shovel and started to clear away more space.

Nate stopped him. "Much as I don't want to, we still have to call the authorities. It's too close to the crime scene."

"It's very close," Eric agreed. "But it's outside the cordon tape so the fine line of the law is on our side. We can call when we're sure we have something to report."

Doc protested. "We don't want to trample on any evidence nor do we want to alienate the authorities." He looked squarely at Nate. "You know the rules."

Nate didn't look happy, Eric thought, but he certainly looked as if he knew the rules Doc referred to.

Nate disappeared outside; Doc followed.

Ruth stepped closer to the tiny opening and peered down. "A root cellar? Did you know it was there?"

"No, I had no idea. I'd have told the police. My sister, Mary, never mentioned it, either. This root cellar's been out of commission for decades, if not a century." Eric carefully stepped into the hole, maneuvering his way around the dirt that still needed to be cleared away.

"I agree," Doc said, coming back into the shed. "None of us knew this existed."

Ruth took a notebook from her bag and went outside. She settled down on a rock beside Nate. He put away his cell phone and actually looked willing to talk. "This find probably isn't connected to the bodies," he surmised.

"Then why do we have to call the sheriff?"

"It's his crime scene. I'm the interloper. And, as a good interloper, I know that no stone goes unturned. If we don't call him, they'll say we purposely hid things. Think about it. If you'd hide a root cellar, you'd hide other things, as well."

Sheriff Mallery arrived alone almost an hour later. He glared at Eric, Ruth and Doc, who'd taken up their usual positions on the porch and walked to the shed checking to see if the cordon tape had been crossed and his crime scene tampered with.

"He wouldn't notice anything amiss if it fell on his head," Ruth muttered.

Eric disagreed. He thought the sheriff plenty smart. Smart enough to make sure this case went the way he wanted, no matter what. Smart enough to keep his name separate enough from the Santellises to wind up sheriff.

Sheriff Mallery made a phone call next, walking away from the shed for a signal. Eric wondered who he called. He looked more than worried, which didn't make sense. The root cellar and the bodies couldn't possibly have anything to do with each other. All the root cellar and the bodies had in common was their inability to stay hidden.

The sheriff finally went back to nose around the shed as if he was checking out something important. Standing up, Eric started for the man.

"The sins of some men are obvious...the sins of others trail behind them." The verse came to Eric and slipped past his tongue before he could call it back. Luckily, the sheriff was only just now walking toward the porch.

"Not sure the sheriff would appreciate you spouting the Bible at him," Doc said as they reached Mallery, who blocked the door to the shed. "That Proverbs or Psalms?"

"Timothy," Nate supplied.

"*You* know the Bible?" Ruth stared at Eric in shock. The sheriff looked taken aback, too.

"I went to parochial school," Eric said, surprised that he felt the need to defend himself, and at the same time somewhat surprised he'd credit parochial school with his knowledge of the Word. Parochial school hadn't introduced him to the Lord, his mother had. Both school and his mother had fought a losing battle of good versus evil thanks to the long shadow of his father.

It had been prison, of all places, where he'd finally gotten acquainted with the Lord. Hours alone in a cell with limited resources—the Bible being one—had given him more than enough time with the Word.

What Eric didn't share with Ruth was that his knowledge of the Word didn't translate into acceptance. No, Eric had a hard time understanding a God who allowed so much evil to exist.

The sheriff simply shook his head and glanced back, clearly annoyed at the hole that had appeared in the middle of his crime scene.

"Funny your investigators didn't find this, Rich Mallery," Doc remarked.

"I'd call this a bit below the beaten path." Mallery defended himself.

"Let's not wait another hundred years," said Nate. "Sheriff, can we go ahead and keep digging?"

"Just the opening," the sheriff huffed.

Ruth picked up the shovel first. With an uneasy look at the sheriff, she jabbed at the hard dirt and muttered, "Hope we don't find another body."

With a pointed look at Eric, the sheriff stated, "Every time one of you Santellises shows up, you leave a path of destruction. I'm going to see to it that the next time you wind up behind bars, you're there for life."

Ruth recognized white-hot anger when it stared her in the face. She was glad she held the shovel and not Eric. Had she been the sheriff, she might have taken a step back, out of harm's way, away from those eyes.

The last week, sitting on the porch, watching the investigation into her husband's death, hadn't given her much time to experience the real Eric Santellis. No, what she had been seeing, what she'd gotten used to, was the well-behaved Eric. She'd forgotten he was a Santellis and a beast waited below the surface. She saw the beast now. The anger enveloped him so quickly he almost staggered.

She stepped back, caught herself—she'd already made

this mistake with Rosa—and instead, after handing the shovel to Nate, went toward Eric. Funny, her feet moved easily. She should feel terrified. But, for some reason, she trusted Eric. It made no sense.

Yes, Ruth was used to witnessing anger, thanks to her father and thanks to many of the men she'd arrested for crimes so heinous she almost cried while filing the reports, while testifying, while in bed at night—alone. Yes, she was used to witnessing anger, but this time—somehow— she knew how to dispel it.

"Eric, don't…" Ruth spoke in a gentle voice, as she did with Megan after a bad dream. Reaching out, she touched his arm.

And just as quickly as the anger came, it went. Eric started to breathe again. He also started to move toward her.

That's when her cell phone rang, saving Ruth from having to deal with a type of intimacy she didn't know how to handle.

"Hello." Ruth spoke into the phone, noticing that her voice seemed unnaturally high-pitched, but then, these were not normal times; why should she sound normal?

It took her a moment to focus on the words coming through the phone, on the world outside the shed, and then she felt terrible. Glancing at her watch, the truth dawned. It was well after three. She could only stutter, "Oh, I'm so sorry. I can't believe I— No, call my mother. She'll come to get Megan. What? You tried? I'll be right there. Thanks, bye." She shoved the phone in her backpack. "I can't believe what time it is or that my cell phone actually picked up a signal in the shed." She tripped over the shovel in her haste to get to the door.

"Megan sick?" Doc asked.

"No, school ended thirty minutes ago. They're waiting for me to pick her up. I—I lost track of time. And they can't get hold of my mother." She handed her flashlight to Eric. "I need to get going. They've allowed her to attend after-school care, but she's not signed up for it."

An hour later, Ruth emptied Megan's backpack. Megan, who hadn't been the least bit bothered by after-school care insisted she wanted to go again. "We sang lots of songs."

"Did you know any of them?" Ruth asked.

"No, they're not from cartoons. We sang an *A* song because we're going to start learning about the letter *A*. It talks, you know. It says three things. *Aa* like apple. Then, there's *aw*. That's what you would say if you took a bite of an apple and there was a worm inside. Finally there's just plain old *A. A. A. A*, like apron."

"Is that right?"

"Yup." Megan nodded. "Did you find the note about what to send tomorrow?"

"I have it right here." Ruth had already read it twice. Seemed homework started on day one at Gila City Elementary. Tomorrow Megan needed three items that began with the letter *A*, plus Ruth was supposed to send a pair of blue shorts, as well as $12.50 for a school T-shirt so Megan would be ready for physical-education class.

"We do have apples?" Megan asked looking concerned.

"Always."

"Not always."

Megan was right. The last two weeks had been unusual. Together, Ruth and Megan packed an apple, one of

Grandma's aprons and one of Megan's drawings from the refrigerator. "Tell your teacher this is art," Ruth advised.

Megan didn't much like the fact that art sounded like it started with *R* but she knew better than to argue with her mother, so she easily changed the subject. "Momma, why are you so dirty?"

Dust-crested shoes, dust-coated pants, a dirty shirt, Ruth suddenly wondered what her face looked like and if anybody besides Megan had noticed. The after-school care woman hadn't said anything, and Ruth had assumed the quizzical look had more to do with Ruth's lateness.

"Were you helping Grandma garden?"

A perfect out, and one Ruth would have taken a few months ago before Sam and Rosa and the Bible interfered. "No, I wasn't helping Grandma."

Megan opened her mouth, closed it, waited a moment and then asked, "Where is Grandma?"

"Ah." Seemed as though Ruth was doing a lot of "ahh-ing" today; must have something to do with the letter *A*. What a time for her mother to disappear. "I don't know. I saw her this morning. I'm sure she's all right. She's probably visiting with one of her friends. Her car's gone."

While Megan ran to put her backpack by the front door so they wouldn't forget it in the morning, Ruth took the phone and headed for the kitchen. After she started boiling the spaghetti, she tried her mother's cell number.

No answer.

She poured the sauce in a pot and called Rosa.

No answer.

She laid the garlic bread on top of aluminum foil, stuck it in the oven, called directory assistance and then dialed the Winters's cabin.

No answer.

She knew Eric had a cell phone; he'd used it to call Rosa the day they'd found Dustin's body. She should have asked for the number. They'd sat on that porch for a week watching the authorities wreak havoc. She'd held a notebook with the title Santellis on the cover, and she didn't have the wherewithal to ask for his number. Two weeks off the job and she was already losing her edge.

Not good.

The authorities, no doubt, had his number. It would take just a call to any one of Gila City's finest—maybe Sam—and she'd have the number in a matter of minutes. She'd also have to answer a barrage of questions.

One thing for sure, Eric, the hermit, would answer. The only time he left the cabin was to buy supplies, and for some reason he drove all the way to Wickenburg to do that. Megan saved her from having to make a decision— to call or not to call—by entering the kitchen.

"Spaghetti! Wish it started with *A*."

"We'll send some to school on *S* day," Ruth promised.

Megan added a plate at Grandma's place, and Ruth felt humbled. She didn't have as much confidence in her mother as Megan did. Yet, she should. Carolyn George had never deserted Ruth. The disappearing act had started the month after Dustin failed to return home. Before that, through everything, she'd been a buffer and a friend.

Friend?

Not really a word Ruth was comfortable with. Growing up, in elementary school and junior high, most kids had been warned away from her. Now that she was a mother, she understood why. She'd hesitate to let Megan spend much time around a friend who had a violent father. Back then, she'd blamed herself. She was too skinny, too freckled, too much of a redhead. But, oh, how she wanted a friend, and her mother had tried. Mom jumped rope, played hopscotch and finger painted. It had *almost* been enough.

In high school, for some reason, the barriers fell away. Kids were too self-involved to listen to parents, and it wasn't hard to let a quiet kid—one who always had her homework done and was willing to share—hang around the circle.

It was her sophomore year, just after Thanksgiving, at lunchtime, when Dustin Atkins looked her way.

He'd called her cute and snatched an apple—*Aah, A, Aw*—from her lunch tray. Where she got the courage to chase after him, she'd never know.

For the next week, Dustin grinned at her whenever she sat at the next lunch table. Then, the next week, he sat at her lunch table. Oh, not next to her, but close enough.

Finally, after about a month, everyone knew to save the spot next to her for him. Her first love, her only love. He was a senior, two years older, and he didn't have a clue how different their worlds were. He lived with June and Ward Cleaver clones. He didn't have a clue what it was like to have an alcoholic, verbally abusive father.

He'd taken her home for dinner right before Christmas. She'd borrowed an outfit from one of her new friends. It had been red pants, a white top with red ribbing and then a Christmas sweater. She'd felt like an imposter when she walked into their living room. She'd acted as if two parents, standing at the door welcoming her, was normal. She'd worked hard not to gawk at the pictures on the wall, at the father who not only poured iced tea for company but who also knew how to play a game of pool afterward without saying a single cuss word when she beat him, and at the brother who drove all the way home from college just to meet his little brother's first real girlfriend.

Billy had called her cute at that dinner.

She'd fallen in love with Dustin, she'd fallen in love with his family and she'd fallen in love with life.

"Mama, the spaghetti sauce is flying." Megan's words brought Ruth back to the present, a few splatters too late.

So it was. The stove would certainly be a joy to clean tonight. Spaghetti sauce dotted the side of the refrigerator, dripped down the front of the stove and even dotted the floor. Ruth drained the spaghetti, put the sauce in a bowl and took out the overbrown, overcrispy garlic bread.

"Grandma doesn't like the bread burned."

"Well, Grandma's not here." The words came out a bit harsher than Ruth intended. The day was catching up with her. Quickly putting the food on the table, she grabbed the milk from the refrigerator and poured.

"When will Grandma be home?" Megan climbed in her chair and waited.

"I don't know." Ruth set the milk on the table before spooning spaghetti on both their plates, poured sauce on top, sat down and picked up her fork.

And stared at it for a minute, thinking.

The first time her mother had disappeared had been right after Dustin's cruiser had been located on Prospector's Way. Megan had just turned three, so she didn't remember. For the next year, Mom had drifted a few times, always to a friend's house, always somewhere Ruth could easily find her. Then, about a year ago, she'd settled down and didn't seem to need the disappearing act anymore.

Ruth finally twirled spaghetti around the fork. "We can't wait for Grandma. The food will get cold."

Megan frowned. "But we forgot to pray."

"Oh." Had they been praying the last two weeks? The weeks after Jose's death, Dustin's discovery and Rosa's suspected involvement. Numbness and anger had carried Ruth through a difficult time. Surely she'd remembered to pray. Obviously they had or Megan wouldn't be acting so affronted at the thought of *not* praying. "Honey, you say it."

Megan bowed her head. "Thank You for this meal. Thank You for hurts that heal. Thank You for my day. Thank You for showing me the way. Amen." Megan raised her head, started to pick up her fork, and then dropped it. "Oops." She bowed her head again. "Please send Grandma home."

"Thank you, Megan." It was working again: the power of prayer Sam and Rosa claimed was so healing. Maybe they were right.

What had Megan said? Thank You for hurts that heal.

THIRTEEN

The next morning, the piece of art that had spent the night in Megan's backpack reappeared on the refrigerator door. Megan clearly was unwilling to count art as a legitimate *A* item. One would think that a simple scan of the house would reveal multiple items beginning with *A*, but no, nothing appeared worthy. Trying to keep all thoughts of Eric's root cellar at bay so she could concentrate on what Megan needed, Ruth pulled out the dictionary and as the minute hand crept ever closer to the time they should leave, she and Megan sat on the couch and started looking for the perfect *A* offering.

Megan liked the sound of Aardvark but they didn't have one. Ruth liked the sound of Aardwolf, mostly because she'd never heard of one. They finally settled on an afghan Grandma had crocheted back when Megan was a few weeks old. It fulfilled the *A* requirement in Megan's eyes and, thanks to an interesting stain and some unraveling yarn, came with a more interesting history than the apple or the apron.

Megan, in all her innocence, assumed Grandma was in her bedroom still asleep. Ruth knew different.

Grandma hadn't come home last night.

That more than anything kept Ruth's mind off what the others might have discovered in the root cellar.

Hustling Megan to the car, Ruth tried to push her worry aside and put on a happy face for her daughter. Kindergarten, what a special year, one that should be full of sticky hands, crayoned pages and making new best friends. Not one that should be cluttered with funerals, missing grandmothers and mothers so filled with angst that their hands shook while buckling a daughter's seat belt.

The school's parking lot wasn't as crowded this morning. Only half the kindergarten parents figured day two deserved the same attention as day one. This time Ruth found a spot on the actual school grounds. Tia pulled in alongside her and called, "Morning!"

"Back at you!"

Manny jumped from the backseat, not willing to wait for his mother to unsnap *his* seat belt, ran around the car, Tia at his heels, and skidded by Megan's door.

Megan frowned.

Tia scolded. "No running in the parking lot. You know better."

"I brought an apple!" Manny announced, digging in his backpack and pulling it out.

Megan's face fell. Ruth quickly opened the door, undid the seat belt—she had a feeling this would be the last morning Megan would allow help—and pulled her daughter from the car.

"Mo-om."

"We're not going home for another *A* item. Lots of your classmates will be bringing apples. Look, Manny brought a green apple. Yours is red. Tell Miss Forest to sort the apples by color and size. You'll have fun."

Megan looked doubtful. She'd perfected the look during the last month. It was called growing up.

Miss Forest had the letter *A* written on the board both lowercase and uppercase. She also had bright shiny apples waiting on the children's desks. The apples had fake eyes, smiles and some even had hair. Megan's had a little pink scarf.

"She's not thinking ahead," Tia whispered.

"What do you mean?" Ruth whispered back.

"Well, when it comes time to celebrate Johnny Appleseed, she'll have used up all her good ideas."

Okay, it was all right to smile, even if it hurt. After all, she was standing in her daughter's kindergarten classroom, surrounded by letter cutouts and apples with black felt marker smiles on them, and watching her daughter blend in with all the other children.

The right clothes, the right smile, the right family.

It was all right to smile even if it felt wrong. After all, she was the only parent who'd buried a husband last week and had a missing mother this morning.

Turning her thoughts to the shed, she wondered if they'd found yet another body?

Ruth knew all her mother's local friends, and Carolyn hadn't been to see any of them. Broken Bones was the next logical step. Ruth *really* wanted to be there, but not because she was searching for her mother. She wanted to be searching for Dustin's killer.

A quick cell-phone call to Pixie Butler, a good friend to her mother, only caused Pixie to worry because, *no,*

Carolyn had not stopped by or called in over a month. There was also Tamela Pruitt. Ruth didn't have her phone number, nor did she know where the Pruitts lived, but she'd find out. Mom used to clean Axel Pruitt's bar. That was it for Carolyn's contacts in Broken Bones. During their time in Broken Bones, Carolyn cleaned and kept a low profile. Ruth had attended school and kept a low profile. *Sometimes the people who kept low profiles knew the most.*

Ruth left the interstate and entered the dirt road that jutted to the left and went the few miles before sighting the town's welcome sign. The town was straight ahead, another five miles away. Ruth hated Broken Bones.

"Let your eyes look straight ahead, fix your gaze directly before you." Proverbs. They'd been studying the fourth chapter. She wished she were in Bible class and studying the Word today. Instead, she fixed her gaze on what was directly before her. Axel's Bar. It was closed.

Axel Pruitt must be pushing the century mark. He'd looked as if he was a hundred back when she'd sat, many an afternoon, on the sidewalk in front of the mud-brown building waiting for her dad to come out.

Just one block away from Axel's Bar was the two-story jail. Ruth knew it well. She hadn't needed to wait on the sidewalk; there'd been a waiting room inside, and old John Tucker, the sheriff twenty years ago, had always handed her a stick of gum. He said it lasted longer than candy. He'd been a smart man; she'd often sat in the waiting room for hours.

It was a start. Ruth could not only get the Pruitts' phone number or address, but she could also take a moment and look up a few things. After parking, Ruth headed inside.

It had been almost a year since she'd last visited. At a back desk, a deputy was busy writing something. A young woman dressed in a pink shirt and jeans spoke into a mouthpiece while monitoring two computers and filling in a crossword puzzle. She had to be a new employee; she still looked naive. That wouldn't last. A few months of hearing lies, curse words and terrible truths, and this little girl would not only look her age but feel it.

Ruth's birth certificate read twenty-seven. The mirror suggested thirty. She felt forty.

"May I help you," the girl finally said.

"Sheriff here?" Ruth asked, more in hopes that he wasn't so she could avoid him.

"He's not available."

Laying her badge on the counter, Ruth said, "I'd like to look at some public records."

A grubby-looking man entered the police station, waved at the girl and disappeared through a door. Disconnecting her headset, the girl made a face in the man's direction, took a paper off her desk and handed it to Ruth.

The cop in her wanted to ask who the man was; the on-somebody-else's-turf in her prevented the words. Ruth wrote her name on the request form, and the girl's eyebrows rose.

"Ruth Atkins? Ricky's friend? The cop's wife?"

"That's me." Ruth continued filling out the form.

"I'm Ricky's girlfriend, Julia. He talks about you all the time. At first, I kinda worried that he had a crush on you, but I know better now."

Ah, Ruth did, indeed, remember. Julia had filled Ricky in on the original phone call from Eric. Clearly, Julia was too young to understand the concept of Loose Lips Sink

Ships. And, since her loose lips put Ruth on the crime scene during its beginning stage, Ruth had no right to complain or scold. Instead, she said, "Yeah, Ricky and I go way back."

Julia started to say more, but happened to look down when Ruth slid the request form across to her. "You know, you're the second person asking for his files. Just who is this Darryl George?"

"He—he w-was my father." Surprise more than anything caused Ruth to stutter.

"Oh, then Carolyn George must be your mother?"

"My mother was here? *She* asked for these files?"

"Yes, this morning. She stayed almost two hours."

Ruth suddenly felt weak. What was her mother up to? "Besides my father's, whose file did she request?"

"Yano Santellis. You know about him, I bet."

"I do," Ruth agreed. She'd gone over his file with a fine-tooth comb three years ago.

"You want Yano's file, too?" Julia asked.

"Yes." If Carolyn had been looking at it, then Ruth intended to look at it, too.

Julia retrieved the files. She was so impressed with actually meeting one of Ricky's friends that she let Ruth use an empty desk. Ruth sat down and waited a moment before opening Yano's file. She then placed her father's next to it, and started the daunting task of comparing dates. It took her just twenty minutes to find what her mother had been checking.

Yano had been picked up for questioning in 1982 for racketeering. He hadn't been arrested. Judging by the paperwork Ruth figured that Yano had been behind a "Pay me or your business will burn down in the morning" operation. Yano issued the orders; he wasn't arrested. People who issue orders seldom leave behind fingerprints.

Her father obeyed the orders and occasionally left fingerprints.

FOURTEEN

Standing on the porch watching Nate and Rich Mallery argue, Eric recognized a dying crime scene when he saw one. The rule of thumb was solve the crime in forty-eight hours or forget it. Dustin Atkins's twenty-four hours was years ago. Lucille Straus's forty-eight hours was up three months ago. Even their discoveries were now growing cold.

The specialists the sheriff had called yesterday were packing up and mumbling about a waste of time. The root cellar was not connected to the crimes. Nate didn't want them to leave. He had plenty of suggestions, ideas, insights, things he'd discovered in the last week that he wanted to discuss, but the sheriff didn't want Nate's help.

Nate was Rosa's man, according to the sheriff.

Nate was impartial. He just wanted the truth. But the argument didn't work. So Nate grumbled and joined Eric on the porch. He'd done what he could on-site; now he'd be looking for answers somewhere else. Still, he wanted to see the root cellar just in case the state investigators had left some stone unturned.

"They say what they found?" Eric asked.

"Old tools, a few items of clothing and some mining paraphernalia."

"But—"

"I know," Nate said. "You'd think a root cellar would have a few remnants of canned goods. I don't know what to think. This is the strangest case I've ever worked on. Nothing feels right. Not those bodies, not the root cellar and certainly not that sheriff." He cleared his throat and stood up, moving toward his Jeep and still shaking his head. Clearly, he'd said too much.

"I think the Mallerys are involved," Eric finally said. "They're connected with my family."

Nate didn't even blink. "We know that. We're investigating both the sheriff and his brother, Benjamin, but so far, nothing."

It was more information than Eric expected, and it renewed his quest to clear Rosa. If Nate couldn't find anything, Rosa must be getting worried. Eric needed a plan.

After slamming the back door of the Jeep, Nate walked toward the sheriff. "Can we go in yet?"

"What do you think you'll find?"

"More than you." Nate had dropped all pretense of professional courtesy.

The sheriff glared. "We're still investigating. Can't have you messing with—"

"I," Nate emphasized, "know my way around a crime scene. Besides, you'd have to sort through all the trespassing and shedding done by the crowd you gathered."

Nate turned to Eric. "I'll be filing a report with Sam and Rosa tomorrow—"

"I'd like a copy of that report," the sheriff said.

"Me, too," said Eric.

"Talk to Sam and Rosa." Nate jumped into his Jeep and said to Eric, "I'm heading for town. I'll be back later this week to see that root cellar. I want to dig deeper."

A minute later, the Jeep disappeared. Unfortunately, the cloud of dust it created continued. Another vehicle came into view. Eric and the sheriff watched until a teenager in a truck passed.

"Too much traffic on this road," the sheriff muttered.

"Why does that bother you? You don't live on Prospector's Way."

"It bothers my brother, and he's as big a pain as your brothers were." Glaring, the sheriff stepped closer. "What do you think about selling this place? I'll give you a fair price. You can go somewhere, start over, man."

"No thanks."

"You're not too bright." The sheriff looked as though he wanted to say more, wanted to strong-arm, just plain wanted to hit something—namely Eric. Instead he stuffed his hands in his pockets and headed for his cruiser, sat inside and made a call.

An hour later, Eric's place was deserted. Whatever state agency Rich Mallery had contacted about the root cellar had finally packed up and disappeared in just under an hour. Eric thought it should have taken all day. It would have taken Nate all day, if he thought the root cellar was connected to the crime, but then he'd have been messing with his tape measure, Ziploc bags and gloves.

And finally Eric was alone. This time, he didn't feel alone. This time he had things to do, things that would help both Rosa and Ruth. First, since the root cellar was right here in his backyard, he'd start investigating. Then, he wanted to find out what motivated the sheriff to make an offer on the cabin.

And even stranger was that this wasn't the first offer to buy the cabin. When Eric exited Florence Prison, he'd carried with him a piece of mail that didn't come from lawyers or reporters.

The white envelope had been from the Broken Bones Real-Estate Office. Apparently, some corporation was willing to fork over a half mil for the property. In some ways, Eric credited the offer with helping him decide where to settle. If he owned property worth a half mil, he needed to know about it. At first, he hadn't been curious about the corporation. Once he saw the property and the shape it was in, he was more curious, but within days he had more pressing matters—two dead bodies—to worry about. Now he figured Sheriff Mallery had been behind the corporation offering to buy the place.

Something to look into… But, right now, there were more important things to do than dwell on unexpected real-estate ventures…like heading for the shed and going down into the root cellar.

Before he could take a step, he saw the smoke signal of an oncoming vehicle. He waited, amazed at how eager he was for company. Ruth's company. Instead, he settled for Doc. The elderly man looked tired. Today, instead of parking, exiting and throwing out the usual greeting of "Anything going on?" Doc slowly left the car and looked around. "Sheriff gone?"

"About an hour ago."

Doc shook his head. "How about all those specialists he called in?"

"They're gone, too."

"Heard they went down in that cellar and didn't find a thing to help their case?"

"You sure hear things fast."

"Small town."

"Not that small."

"Boy, you have no idea."

Come to think of it, Eric thought, bad news traveled this fast back in Phoenix, too. All a member of his family had to do was sneeze and the anchor on the five o'clock news said, "Bless you."

"I'm going to go explore. You coming with me?" Eric asked. Truth be told, he was glad to have Doc with him to chase away the ghosts of his ancestors.

"I wouldn't miss it," Doc said, and yawned.

Careful to avoid the crime scene, they stepped into the shed and headed for the entrance. Eric took a moment to find Doc a flashlight and himself a lantern.

"Steps safe?" Doc aimed the beam into the darkness. "They probably haven't been used in a while."

Eric held his lantern carefully and took one step at a time. There was no railing, and the lantern definitely wasn't a beacon. "They're narrow but seem secure. Look, we don't have to do this today. You look beat."

"Wife had a rough night, but I'm all right."

Eric made it all the way to the bottom before Doc took his first step.

"You need some help?" Eric called up.

"No, I'm just trying to get my bearings."

Soon, but not soon enough, both men stood in a room awash in history. Nate's assessment was lacking a bit. The root cellar was about the same size as the shed. It smelled of dirt and dampness and age. Between the glow of the lantern and the flashlight, Eric could make out the clumps of clutter. Sure enough, scattered throughout the room, there were tools. Eric could identify buckets, pickaxes, shovels, rock hammers, screwdrivers, sieves, crevice tools and in the corner one very rusty wheelbarrow.

"Interesting," Doc said. "But it makes sense. Your great-great-grandfather discovered the Riddell Mine alongside the sheriff's great-great-grandfather."

"Yeah, too bad my ancestor couldn't hold on to it."

Back against a wall was a small pile of clothes. Eric squatted and started sorting pants, shirts and hats. Doc aimed the flashlight around the room and then roamed a bit, touching walls and feeling supports. He found a corner he liked, did some investigating and apparently decided there was nothing of interest, so he joined Eric and carefully bent down before picking up a raggedy pair of pants. "Your ancestors were either small men or inclined to dress like a Chinaman. These are made of kemp."

"I'm the shortest of the brothers and I'm six foot one. My father is six foot three. And I think I'd know if I had a Chinaman as an ancestor."

"Well, I've read my wife's book. She says that plenty of Chinese laborers were used in the mine." Doc picked up the raggedy remains of what looked like a shirt. "This is a padded cotton jacket. Red." He fingered the stacks Eric had made earlier. "According to my wife's book, color denotes where the Chinese immigrants originated."

"Why would their stuff be here?"

"That I couldn't even guess at, but I'm thinking Elizabeth would have an idea. I'm heading topside." Doc looked at the stairs and took a breath.

Eric followed Doc up the steps, his interest in what Elizabeth might know passing his curiosity about the root cellar. "You want to call your wife and invite her to come over and take a look?"

"Elizabeth uses a walker now. She's an eighty-year-old woman. She's got seven years on me. I'm only seventy-three." Doc winced. "Guess I'm a pup. Look, why don't you come over for lunch? You think I don't know you exist on cereal made with powdered milk. It's about time you put a real meal in that belly and met Elizabeth."

Temptation reared its head. Leave the cabin, go to the home of a neighbor. No, that's not what Eric planned to do. He'd settled in Broken Bones in order to be alone. Of course, last Sunday taught him just how little he liked being alone. Still, Doc was becoming too much like a friend, and so was Ruth.

"I don't know," Eric said. "I've got a lot to do." *Like fix up a house, solve a murder, be alone.*

Doc exited the shed and blinked against the sunlight. "I guarantee she'll settle your curiosity, as well as fill your stomach. It's Wednesday. We usually have grilled cheese sandwiches and tomato soup."

Eric battled between what was safe and what was sane. "It's just not a good day," he finally managed.

Heading for his car, Doc said, "I've got her book in the backseat. I'm supposed to give you a copy."

"How much?"

"Free. Elizabeth spent almost a decade researching Broken Bones history before she started writing. Then, she spent another decade writing."

"Impressive."

"What's impressive," said Doc, handing over the book

before climbing in and digging out his car keys, "is how much of Broken Bones history is tied in with Santellis and Mallery history."

Unfortunately, Eric knew plenty about his family's history. He really didn't need Mrs. Winters's book. "Broken Bones has spent a century trying to erase the Santellises from their history book. Surely your wife knows that. The sheriff's ancestor left a legacy to be proud of. My ancestor ran out on his wife and family."

"My wife says things are not always what they seem." With that, Doc started the engine and slowly backed away from the cabin.

Okay, Eric wanted, needed, to listen. He wanted to know about his family and the Chinese. He rapped on Doc's window. "Okay, I'll come to lunch. It'll take me a moment to get the car started. I'm pretty sure I'm out of gas." He'd only taken one step toward his truck when another cloud of dust appeared on the horizon. After a few minutes, Ruth's silver SUV came around the corner.

"The good thing about grilled cheese and soup is you never run out." Doc called out the driver's-side window. "Tell Ruth to come along."

"Not so fast!" Eric sprinted from his car to Doc's. "I don't know where you live."

"You don't?" Doc honestly looked confused. "We're in the cabin on the other side of the Mallerys' place."

"You're that close?"

"Yup, only a half mile uphill on Prospector's Way."

"I didn't know."

"Lot you don't know. Our home belonged to Elizabeth's parents. She's never lived anywhere else."

"She knew my grandfather?"

"And his father." Doc started to roll up the driver's-side window.

Ruth didn't wave as she passed Doc and skidded to a stop by Eric. Her tires were a bit too close for comfort. That was his first clue that he had a somewhat distraught female on his hands. Rolling down the passenger-side window, she tersely asked, "Anything going on?"

Her eyes were red and snapping. He had only one sister, but one was enough to know that the wrong word would instigate a rampage of tears. "This morning the officials said the root cellar is in no way connected to the murders. Nate says he's all done here. He left. Doc and I explored the root cellar. Lots of old mining tools down there and lots of clothing we figure belonged to the Chinese."

She wiped away an errant tear before she picked up a green notebook. In a shaky hand, she made an annotation before abruptly asking, "What are you doing next?"

The fact that he was attracted to this woman amazed him in so many ways. In truth, he'd never seen her happy. His impression of her all had to do with mourning, denial, determination and now anger.

"I'm heading over to the Winters's. They've invited me—us—to lunch. Ruth, are you all right?" It was a lame question, he knew, but it was the only question he could think to ask.

She pursed her lips. "Has my mother been by to ask you any questions?"

"Your mother?"

"Yes, my mother!"

"Why would your mother stop by here?"

"Maybe to ask you not to tell me that my father used to work for yours."

FIFTEEN

She could tell by the look on his face that he knew nothing about it. What surprised her most was that she *believed* the look.

Believed a Santellis.

Well, in truth, he was as much a victim of a parent's actions as she was. "When was this?" he finally said.

"The eighties."

"Oh, sure, I'd remember that," he said snidely, but then his voice gentled. "I was just a teenager."

"And I was in grade school," she said softly.

"When did you find this out?"

"This morning."

"How?"

"I stumbled across the information while looking for my mother. She left sometime yesterday morning and didn't come back."

"Did you call the police?"

Ruth couldn't help it. She gave him exactly the look she often gave Megan when Megan said something completely off the wall. "I am the police."

Before Eric had a chance to do or say anything, Ruth

continued, "My mother spent some time at the Broken Bones sheriff's office this morning going over old arrest reports. I asked for the same reports." She shook her head. "You know, three years ago I sat at that sheriff's office for weeks reading every word written about your brothers and father, I was so sure they were behind Dustin's disappearance, but it never occurred to me to ask for my own father's file."

She gripped the steering wheel tightly, until her knuckles turned white.

He noticed. "You want a drink? I can get you a bottled water."

She wasn't thirsty, she didn't want to come in, but she did turn the car engine off and kept talking. "He worked for your father. While we lived here, he worked for your father." Her voice fell to a whisper. "My father is exactly like your father."

"Probably not." The hard expression that had so defined his eyes a moment ago vanished. "No one is like my father. Just exactly what did your father do?"

"Racketeering. He bullied local businesses into paying a safety fee."

"To keep my dad from destroying their property," Eric guessed.

"My father delivered the ultimatum and carried the match."

"Ruth, you do realize that you can't blame yourself for what your father was?"

"I do realize that. I'm just so mad I spent so much time judging others for something I'm guilty of, too. I'm like that man in the Bible."

"What man?"

"The one who had the plank."

"Ah." Eric nodded. "You know, I think Jesus was talking to the people who were well aware that they had a plank in their eye."

Ruth felt humbled. Standing before her was a man who truly didn't have a plank in his eye, although he, of all people, probably had earned the right to have one. The compassionate look in his eyes turned to concern. It disconcerted Ruth, this ability to read his expression. She almost felt as if she was intruding, eavesdropping, on a piece of the man best kept hidden.

"You're too tough on yourself." He continued, "And you need to get over your father. Hating him will drive you nuts. Believe me, I know."

She knew it, too. She'd hated her father for so long. Then, Dustin came along and taught her forgiveness, but it must have been a superficial forgiveness. Otherwise, it would have lasted even after his death.

She was certainly one volatile female: angry one minute, sad the next and then melancholy. Well, maybe she had a right to be: she'd buried her husband, lost a mother and found out her father willingly played footsie with the Santellises. No, she wasn't having a good day.

Truthfully, he wanted to go to Doc's, find out whatever he could about the Chinese and the Mallery-Santellis family history, and then get busy helping clear Rosa. Instead, he said, "You want me to help you look for your mother?"

"No, she's done this before. And since she was just at the police station this morning, I'm not worried that something's happened to her. I just want her back where

GET 2 FREE BOOKS!

HURRY!

Return this card promptly to get **2 FREE Books** *and* **2 FREE Bonus Gifts!**

Love Inspired.
SUSPENSE

YES! *Please send me the 2 FREE Love Inspired® Suspense books and 2 FREE gifts for which I qualify. I understand that I am under no obligation to purchase anything further, as explained on the back of this card.*

affix
free
books
sticker
here

323 IDL EL4Z   **123 IDL EL3Z**

FIRST NAME   LAST NAME

ADDRESS

APT.#   CITY

STATE/PROV.   ZIP/POSTAL CODE

Steeple
Hill®

Steeple Hill Reader Service™—Here's How It Works:

Accepting your 2 free books and 2 free gifts places you under no obligation to buy anything. You may keep the books and gifts and return the shipping statement marked "cancel." If you do not cancel, about a month later we will send you 4 additional books and bill you just $3.99 each in the U.S. or $4.74 each in Canada, plus 25¢ shipping & handling per book and applicable taxes if any.* That's the complete price, and — compared to cover prices of $4.99 each in the U.S. and $5.99 each in Canada — it's quite a bargain! You may cancel at any time, but if you choose to continue, every month we'll send you 4 more books, which you may either purchase at the discount price...or return to us and cancel your subscription.

*Terms and prices subject to change without notice. Sales tax applicable in N.Y. Canadian residents will be charged applicable provincial taxes and GST. All orders subject to approval. Books received may not be as shown. Credit or debit balances in a customer's account(s) may be offset by any other outstanding balance owed by or to the customer. Please allow 4 to 6 weeks for delivery.

she belongs." Ruth picked up a notebook and stared past Eric and down the road that led to town. "It's not like she's hiding, but more like she's hiding something."

"I'm heading to Doc's for lunch. You're invited."

"Good. They're on my list. Mom used to clean their house. She considered Elizabeth a friend. But first can I see the root cellar?"

In a matter of minutes, Eric again breathed the dust of history. Exploring the root cellar with Ruth was a whole different animal than exploring it with Doc. Doc had been at first hesitant and then eager to leave. Ruth was sure-footed. It took him only a moment to realize Ruth had three mantras. One, who needs a flashlight? Two, why take one step at a time when three will do? And, three, who says dirt and grime are to be avoided?

"I always start at the beginning," she announced. So, she started at the beginning: the steps. "They're double stacked and shored up by steel. Whoever installed them expected heavy use." Wall by wall, corner by corner, Ruth went over the room. "This was a utilized cellar. Look at how packed down the earth is. Yep, lots of traffic. So much that not even years of nonuse changed the makeup." She knelt, then sat down cross-legged— not even caring that the seat of her pants got dirty—and picked up a darkened object. It was a fork. A few minutes later she'd uncovered more utensils. Then, she separated the clothes from blankets and muttered, "People slept down here."

"Maybe the Chinese?" Eric suggested. He showed her the padded jacket and explained about the pants being made of kemp. He could also see her fingers itching to write the information in one of those notebooks of hers.

She'd need more light. She left the clothing and headed for a wall. She paused, so quiet he could imagine the sound of her breathing. He followed and wound up standing so close to her he was surprised she didn't jump.

"Someone, or maybe lots of someones, scratched into this wall." She ran her fingers over the grooves. "No, they didn't just scratch. They raked their fingernails, dug deep. Look at this. Someone wanted out."

"Out where?"

She shrugged. "Who knows?"

"Well, they must have gotten out. The forensic team would have mentioned more bones."

Her snort resembled a laugh. "You see anything else questionable?" Eric asked.

"Yes." Ruth looked over at the wheelbarrow. "Why is that here? One, who in their right mind would attempt narrow stairs juggling a wheelbarrow? And, two, what good is a wheelbarrow in a root cellar? It doesn't make sense."

"Storage?" Eric suggested.

Ruth frowned and shook her head.

"You think Elizabeth Winters might know why the wheelbarrow's down here, as well as the Chinese clothing?" Eric asked.

"Why do you bring her up?"

"It's something we can ask her while we eat lunch. Doc said she might have some insight."

Ruth's eyes lit up. "Okay, let's head out. I'm getting hungry, and I'm all for killing two birds with one stone." She was out of the root cellar and to her vehicle before Eric had a chance to gather his lantern and close the shed's door. As he stepped into the sunlight, he squinted. She was in her SUV and waiting for him.

Nope, no way would a woman like Ruth be waiting for him. It was the Santellis curse. No way a good woman wanted to be involved with him. Rosa had and look what it cost her. Two years of her life and now maybe a life sentence.

"Hey! Are you coming?" Ruth leaned over and opened the passenger-side door. "Get in. I've got to come back this way anyhow."

He got in and pushed aside her notebooks, a doll, a Bible and a box of tissues. She chewed her bottom lip and looked at him. He wished his close proximity didn't make her think twice about offering him a ride but he applauded her wisdom. And what he really wished was that it was his company that made her eyes light up.

Ruth didn't need directions. She pointed her SUV in the direction of the Winterses' place. A few minutes later, a ramshackle cabin came into view. She'd forgotten the Mallerys had a home between the Winterses and Eric.

"Looks a lot like my place," Eric said.

Although she didn't respond, Ruth agreed, right down to the trash strewn across the land and the decrepit shed.

"You suppose there are any bodies in his shed?" Eric asked, half in jest.

"Wouldn't surprise me." Ruth blinked. Sometimes she could almost forget where Dustin had been found—how lost he'd been. Then, the memory came swishing up and brought tears to her eyes. Tears she always blinked away.

Instead of crying, she studied the man sitting on the front porch. She recognized him from this morning at the sheriff's office. He was the oldest Mallery: Benjamin. Of the two Mallery brothers, he was the scary one, and about

Ruth's mother's age. He wore the same pair of overalls and the same ball cap. A high-powered rifle rested next to him. He also held a pair of binoculars and seemed to be aiming them right at her. "You suppose he sits there most of the day watching us?" Ruth mused.

"More likely," Eric said, "he's watching you."

"Me," Ruth squeaked. "Why me?"

"Well, if I owned a pair of binoculars and you were within sight, I'd be watching you."

"Oh," Ruth mustered. But she felt oddly pleased. It had been a long time since someone of the opposite gender had sincerely complimented her looks. For the last two years, the only references about her looks came from the men she arrested, and she didn't consider foul-language-peppered pickup lines as real compliments.

The Winterses' cabin was just a mile past the Mallery place. Ruth took the turn and drove up a graded, sloping driveway and parked. What she saw almost took her breath away. "They've certainly been working on the place," she breathed.

At one time, the Winterses' cabin had resembled Eric's and the sheriff's. All three dwellings were large, two storied, with the second story consisting of a steepled ceiling. Ruth figured Eric's and the Mallerys' places still looked a lot like the way they had a hundred years ago. The Winterses' place no longer looked as it did even twenty years ago when Ruth's mother cleaned for them.

"You gonna sit there forever or get out?" Eric finally said, ending Ruth's foray into the past.

"Yours and the Mallerys' cabins belong to the Zane Grey end-of-the-road era. This one looks like *Lifestyles of the Rich and Famous.*"

"Well, Doc is a doc. They make decent money."

"Back when my mother cleaned for them the place didn't look quite like this. But, even then, compared to your cabin, it was a showplace." Ruth took a breath. This was her dream: a home like this, a place to kick off her shoes and relax. She loved how the cabin had a wrap-around porch. She loved the orange-brown color of the wood. She loved the majestic windows that reflected the view of Rich Hill.

A Christmas tree would look perfect in front of those windows. She could envision Megan sitting underneath the boughs and hugging the dog Ruth always meant to get her.

"Sometimes," Ruth continued, shaking off the day-dreams and returning to reality, "if Mom worked here at night. I'd stay for dinner."

The Winters stepped out on their porch. Doc waved for them to come on up. "About time you got here. You gonna stay out there and gawk forever?" he yelled.

"See?" Eric said. "We've been sitting here too long."

"Men," Ruth muttered, and then admitted to herself it had nothing to do with men and everything to do with her. She didn't want to go into this place from her childhood. On one hand, it was her dream. One that would never be fulfilled now that Dustin was gone. On the other hand, because of where they were, it was like taking a step back into time—a time that hadn't been particularly pleasant.

The Winters's place, back then, had been an all-too-brief reprieve.

What could she call it today?

SIXTEEN

Ruth opened the SUV's door and headed for the stairs leading up to the wraparound porch. "Place really has changed," she commented. What she didn't mention was how much Mrs. Winters had changed, gotten smaller. She was bent. Her once-curly hair was now cut short and straight. Her hands grasped a walker.

"Oh, my," Elizabeth said. "That's the truth. I about died two years ago when they put the front windows in. Used to be I had to sit on the porch for the full effect, now I can sit on the couch."

Doc held open the door. Ruth took a hesitant step in and then let out a sigh of amazement. What she saw looked nothing like what she remembered, except… Over by the fireplace were the pictures. Like a magnet, they drew her, and she moved across the room. Some of the pictures she remembered, but their number had surely multiplied.

"My grandchildren's children," Elizabeth said proudly.

"The shooting trophies are yours?" Ruth picked one up. "I noticed them when I was younger, but I thought they were Doc's."

"My father taught me how to shoot when I was just a girl. Strange to remember now. He'd actually go out and shoot a deer or sometimes even a squirrel. We'd eat it that night. James—" she smiled in Doc's direction "—he's a city boy. Couldn't hit the side of a barn if he tried." She squinted at Ruth. "What made you ask?"

"We saw one of your photos down at the café."

Elizabeth laughed. "I keep telling John Mallery to update his photos but he likes all that old timey stuff. Come on in the kitchen, keep me company while I make the soup. We'll leave the men to their conversation."

They were talking flooring: grain and type.

"James always makes the sandwiches. He claims I burn them." Elizabeth led the way to the kitchen. "Didn't used to be that way. Nowadays I can never remember how long to cook them."

The kitchen was twice the size as before, good thing, too, because the walker fit easily. Now that Ruth could see the back of the house, she realized the remodel included a huge add-on. "Wow."

"I know," Elizabeth said. "I keep pinching myself."

Ruth took a seat at the kitchen table. She carefully moved a frilly place setting and folded her hands. Now that she and Elizabeth were alone, away from Eric's curious ears, she asked, "Have you seen my mother?"

"You mean, recently?" Elizabeth turned on the gas stove and picked up a spoon.

"Within the last twenty-four hours?"

"She's missing? Have you called the police?"

"I'm not calling the police. She disappears every once in a while."

"She never disappeared while you were growing up, did she?"

"No, and I'd remember."

"When did she start disappearing?"

"What?"

"When did she start disappearing?"

"About the time Dustin disappeared," Ruth admitted. "At first I blamed it on my questions about my father, but now I realize she disappears when I mention Dustin."

Elizabeth took three bowls out of a cupboard and set them on the table. "But she always comes back?"

"Yes, she always comes back. Mrs. Winters, do you need any help?"

"No, I need to keep moving. And, since your mother always comes back, then, I guess I'd stop worrying."

"Hah," Ruth said. "I'd stop worrying if every time I turned around I didn't find something to worry about."

Elizabeth smiled. "I do know the feeling."

"I've tried all her friends in Gila City. Then I thought maybe she'd be here in Broken Bones. I stopped by the police station this morning. She'd been there."

Elizabeth paused as she took silverware from a drawer. "Is she in trouble?"

"No, she wasn't arrested, and I don't think she's in trouble," Ruth said. "It's more like she's worried about what I'll find out."

Two spoons fell to the floor. Slowly, but before Ruth could jump up to help, Elizabeth retrieved them. "Find out? Like what?"

"Like about my father working for the Santellises. Eric doesn't know anything. Do you?"

Silverware went on top of the place mats, glasses filled with ice soon joined. A bag of chips appeared in the middle of the table.

"Mrs. Winters, are you going to answer me. Your silence tells me you knew."

"I knew," Elizabeth answered. "Pretty much everybody knew. It's why the other kids in the class stayed away from you."

"Mom should have told me," Ruth muttered.

"When? Back then you were a scared and lonely eight-year-old who didn't even know the Santellises existed. Then, when Carolyn moved in with you two years ago, she couldn't tell you. You blamed the Santellises for your husband's disappearance. Talk about bad timing."

"Why is she so upset now? Upset enough to run?"

"My guess, because of how closely you're working with Eric Santellis."

"He's a good guy!"

"Even good men—" she looked a bit sad "—do bad things."

Before Ruth could reply, the men ventured in. Doc went right to the cupboard, grabbed another bowl and next put out the correct amount of silverware. Finally he went to the fridge and took out bread and cheese. He sprayed butter in the skillet his wife had waiting. Eric washed his hands and sat down next to Ruth while Elizabeth poured iced tea.

"I gave Eric your book this morning," Doc admitted. "We were just discussing it."

Eric slid a book toward Ruth. "Here, take a look."

Ruth opened the first page.

Broken Bones
The Town that Wouldn't Die
and
The People Who Would

"Pretty gloomy," Ruth said. She flipped through the small, brown book quickly. Large print and lots of penciled drawings made it an easy skim.

"The town has a bloody history," Elizabeth said. "I would so love to see your root cellar. The early settlers—that would be your great-great-great grandfather Salvatore—didn't so much use the root cellar for storage but to hide from Indians."

"What was really fascinating," Doc said, "and you'll find this if you read her book, is the Indians would burn the cabins down, and the family would be safe in the root cellar. When the fire died out, the father would go outside, the Indians would see him, and they'd be afraid. Then the father would go back inside, change clothes, come out again, and the Indians would assume different spirits were coming out of the building."

Elizabeth jumped in, "That shed, on your property, is newer than your cabin. The first structure was burned down by Indians. When they rebuilt, your great-great-great grandmother Riza wanted it bigger and closer to the cabin so what you see now is a few yards from the original site."

"You talk as if you knew her," Eric said.

"I didn't know her," Elizabeth said, giving Eric a scorching look that only a third-grade teacher knew how to give. "I'm not that old."

Doc masterfully flipped the sandwiches, pressed them down and then flipped them onto plates with a surgeon's precision. A moment later, a hot sandwich was in Ruth's hand. A few minutes later, most of it was in her stomach, along with the soup. While she ate and half listened to the history of Broken Bones, she flipped through the book. There were chapters on the railroad, on guns, on the Chinese tunnels and so on.

"When I was young," Elizabeth said, "your grandmother was still alive. She had Riza's journals."

"Journals?" Eric perked up.

"I think those journals were what inspired me to write the history of Broken Bones. So much was in them."

"May I see them?" Eric asked.

"They're long gone. I remember the day we lost them. Come to think of it, it was August, like today. We were in town for one of the meet-the-teacher nights. A monsoon came like I'd never seen. We weren't worried. We'd weathered monsoons before. But this one came with a microburst. It peeled a portion of the cabin away. Rain got inside. I had an old chest with my mama's stuff in it. The journals were in it, too. Ruined. I remember holding the torn and sodden pages and weeping."

"Did you write down what you remembered?" Ruth asked.

"Most of it appeared in my book," Elizabeth responded.

"I'd like my own copy, if you have another."

"We'll give you one before you leave. Speaking of that monsoon reminds me, that root cellar might be dangerous. It's old, and with that shed on top, it might all cave in." Elizabeth settled back in her chair. She'd only eaten a spoonful or two of her soup and looked about ready to fall asleep. "You need to fill it in."

"It's pretty sturdy," Ruth said. "I checked."

"What looks sturdy isn't always sturdy." For some reason, Elizabeth looked at her husband, and Ruth caught the essence of something left unsaid.

"Why did we find Chinese clothes and mining tools in the root cellar?" Ruth closed the book. "There's also a place where they dug their nails in the wall as if they were trying to get out. Could they have been down there when the Indians came?"

A glance at her watch told her she had maybe five minutes before she needed to leave.

"No, I don't believe so," Elizabeth said. "Back then the Chinese were considered inferior. They wouldn't be invited to a white man's home. I'll bet the root cellar was used for storage."

"If they used the cellar for storage, why isn't there more of the Santellises' belongings down there?"

"Back then," Elizabeth argued, "they didn't have the abundance we have today. And, what is down there probably did belong to Sal. That would be the mining stuff. He was a founder of the Riddell Mine. He hired the Chinese."

"Okay." Ruth wiped her mouth with a napkin and stood up. "I buy some of this, but not all. There's a huge wheelbarrow down there. It makes no sense."

"Maybe it wound up down there when they were rebuilding and the root cellar's opening was exposed."

Truthfully, Ruth wasn't convinced but had to accept that maybe nobody knew the answer, yet. She gathered her dishes and Eric's and stacked them in the sink after rinsing them. "We really need to get going. Megan's school gets out in an hour."

"You hear anything else about Dustin?" Doc asked, following them to the door.

"No," Ruth admitted. "And I'm starting to feel run ragged."

He stepped to her side and patted her on the shoulder. "Life will do that. Maybe you need to let this go. Let me know if you need anything."

"I will," Ruth said.

Eric shook Doc's hand and headed down the stairs. Ruth held her hand out, too. Doc took it and leaned close. "Ruthie," he said, "there are too many secrets. Your mother needs forgiveness. What she did was a long time ago."

"What *she* did," Ruth repeated slowly.

Doc clutched her hand, tightly, as if afraid she'd fall and he'd need to catch her. "*She* needs your forgiveness. You see, it wasn't just your father who worked for the Santellises. Your mother did, too."

He'd been with her almost every day for two weeks. Sometimes it took longer to get a feel for a woman—not Ruth. He'd felt the connection that first day when she marched from her SUV, all dressed in black and ready to take on the world: namely him. The term, he knew from his Criminal Justice classes, was imprint. She'd left her imprint. *On him.* Before he went to sleep at night, he thought about her sitting on his porch, notebooks in hand, impossible drawings on her paper.

He knew her.

For a moment, watching her with Doc, he thought he saw her knees buckle, and just when he was about to rush back up the stairs to catch her, she seemed to regroup. "What happened?" he asked, the moment she got in the vehicle. She blinked, furiously, but a tear slipped by and then another until it seemed that she could not stop. "Oh, Ruthie."

"Don't call me that." She beat the steering wheel with her hand. Then, slowly, word by word, she said, "We. Are. Not. Friends."

She collapsed then, against the steering wheel, more angry than sad, and crying too hard to do much about either. He glanced at the cabin, but the Winters were inside with the door closed. Something Doc said had to have sparked this crying jag. Getting out of the SUV, he walked to the driver's side. "You want me to carry you to the passenger side?" he asked. He doubted she'd welcome his touch.

"No, I can walk."

And she did, with one hand pressed against the SUV as if she were an old woman and a bitter, cold breeze was pushing against her. Once she buckled in and he started the car, she stared out the window and cried and cried and cried while he drove toward his place. The questions he wanted to ask were silenced by her tears. Today, just like the first day, in his living room when Dustin's body lay in the shed, she didn't make a noise.

About the time he turned into the driveway, her cell phone rang. She took it out of her purse, checked the clock and muttered, "Great, again." Putting it to her ear, she said, "Yes, I'm on my way." She closed the phone and muttered, "I meant to sign her up for after-school care."

She had the door open before he completely stopped the vehicle. She was around the vehicle and tapping her foot in another second. Gallantly, he exited and held the door.

She jumped into the driver's seat and put the SUV in gear before he had time to shut the door. And she looked at him, with such an expression of loss, sorrow, and… something else.

He recognized the look—half invitation, half rebuttal. He'd seen it before on the faces of people who thought him a fairly decent guy until they learned his last name.

She left without saying goodbye.

This time, he wasn't sure she'd be back.

And, now, he truly felt alone.

Pulling his cell phone from his pocket, he walked to the side of the porch where he always got the best reception and called Doc.

"You gonna tell me what you said to her?" Eric bypassed hello.

"She didn't tell you?"

"If she had, I wouldn't need to call you, now, would I?"

Doc cleared his throat. "It's not gonna make you happy."

"You've known me now for two weeks. Tell me one thing that has made me happy."

"The thought of parquet flooring."

"Not funny."

"Okay, son—"

Suddenly, irrationally, Eric understood why Ruth had reacted so negatively to being called Ruthie. He was feeling the same way about Doc calling him son.

"I told her that her mother used to work for your father."

Eric wanted to be surprised. He hated it, the knowing that nothing his family did surprised him. "Doing what?"

"When she cleaned houses, she snooped. She found out who had money, how they got it and when. Then, she told Yano."

"This isn't common knowledge, I take it, or Ruth would have heard it by now."

"No, I'd say there's only a few of us left who know."

"My family, you and..."

"The Mallerys."

SEVENTEEN

Start at the beginning.

Eric first heard the advice from Jimmy Handley. That had been five years ago, and Jimmy had been an undercover police officer bent on ridding Eric's neighborhood of drugs. Eric hated drugs and agreed to help—as long as he wasn't asked to do anything against his family.

Nothing his family did surprised him; everything he did surprised his family.

For almost a year, he and Jimmy followed lead after lead after lead, all on a quest to locate the top drug supplier, and yes, Eric took information from his family. He'd been somewhat relieved to find that his big brother, Tony, wasn't at the top of the drug-supplying food chain. But, then again, if Tony had held that position maybe the war would have ended differently.

When Eric and Jimmy had exhausted all their leads, they looked for more. Eventually they'd found Rosa. Back then she'd been an emergency-room nurse. She'd been easy to enlist. She hated drugs, and she had no qualms about taking down Eric's family. Actually, she'd rather looked forward to it. She'd been Eric's junior-high girlfriend until her older brother died from an overdose. Eric's oldest brother had supplied the drugs.

At Jimmy's urging, she kept a log of people who came into the E.R. because of drug overdoses: what they said and what they'd taken. Working alongside Jimmy and Rosa, for those two years, Eric felt a sense of belonging, a sense of purpose, a sense of rightness. He'd enrolled in the University of Arizona, criminal-justice major, and he'd even started going to church again.

His mother would have liked that.

Then, one night, one life-altering night, at the apartment of a drug dealer, one war ended and another began. Eric and Jimmy had considered this stakeout so "nothing" that they'd brought Rosa along. They wanted to up her contribution; they wanted her seen. That way, the victims flooding E.R. might loosen their tongues a bit more. It wasn't a plan he and Jimmy had liked. And, they never really got to implement it. Because that night, that life-altering night, wouldn't you know it, they'd met up with the top drug supplier.

His name was Cliff Handley.

Jimmy Handley called him Dad.

Had called him Dad for the last time that night.

Seemed crime families worked both sides of the fence. In a drug bust gone horribly wrong, Officer Cliff Handley, highly decorated, a hero, shot his own son.

Not even Eric's dad would have done that.

And when the gunpowder settled, Eric went to jail for the murder of his best friend, Jimmy Handley, and Rosa dropped off the face of the earth, along with a quarter of a million dollars, because there was no one she could trust, neither cop nor crook.

Then, two years later, she met Sam Packard.

The two of them pursued justice and not only brought down Cliff Handley, but also managed to get Eric Santellis released from jail, despite his last name.

It was their proximity, as well as the offers to buy the cabin, that drew him to Broken Bones. It hadn't turned into the beginning Eric had been hoping for, but no one could have foretold what waited for him.

Two bodies in his shed.

A cop's widow who touched his soul as no one else ever had.

And Rosa in danger of being framed for a murder she didn't commit, just like Eric.

Eric needed to discover how and why those bodies got in his shed. Plus, he needed to figure out if Ruth could get past his last name. He needed to start now, today, this minute.

Unearthing a receipt, he started writing on the back.

"Start as if this is a new beginning," Rosa had advised when Eric called to tell her he was settling in Broken Bones in his grandfather's cabin. "It's what I did."

"I always start at the beginning," Ruth had announced this morning when she started down the root cellar stairs.

Eric figured he had two beginnings to choose from. One, the offer to buy his cabin—the one that came in the mail the day he got out of jail, that is. Two, the first body—Lucille Straus.

He started writing:

> Land
> Lucy
> Dustin

Mallerys
Ruth
Nate
Root Cellar

It wasn't much, but it was a beginning.

He pulled his car keys from his back pocket. Ten minutes later, he had filled up his gas tank and was heading in the direction of town and a place called Broken Bones Realty, which turned out to be just a mile or so from the highway turnoff. Broken Bones Realty was housed in a dirty brown building roughly the size of his shed, and one car soaked up the sunshine in a parking lot made of dirt. His truck felt right at home.

The surroundings might be rustic, the business might be falling down around her, but the real-estate agent still sported upswept hair and wore a dark blue suit and heels. She hid her disappointment that he wasn't looking to buy or sell. She didn't hide her disappointment, or fear, when he finally gave his name.

"Eric Santellis," she breathed, and sat down. To her credit, she didn't glance past him as if expecting more goons. She also didn't give him the once-over as if looking for a gun.

"Alive and well."

She swallowed. For the first time, he appreciated his name and the doors, mouths, it opened. She willingly, eagerly, gave him the name of the person behind the company who'd made the offer on his land.

The name surprised him. Expecting to hear Rich Mallery, instead he got the sheriff's brother, Benjamin Mallery—the binocular-toting neighbor.

* * *

Signing Megan up for day care took a good half hour. Ruth hurried through the paperwork. Megan used the time to chase a little boy across the playground. She caught him, too. Ruth applauded and felt her spirits lift, a little.

As they walked to the car—well, Megan skipped— Ruth took a deep breath and tried to release the tension. If the next half of the month continued as the first half, she'd need those anger-management courses again.

Right now, and for the last few days, she'd felt both rushed and cheated. Ruth was starting to believe they'd find Dustin's killer or killers. But, since the funeral, she'd spent less time with Megan. A sudden rush of longing stopped Ruth. She swept Megan up in her arms and hugged her.

"Mommy, you okay?"

"Yes, sweetie. I'm okay." Ruth didn't want quality time with Megan; she wanted all the time in the world with her. Dustin was dead; Megan wasn't.

"Mama, is Grandma home yet?"

"No, honey." Ruth put Megan down. "Grandma's not home yet. That's why I was late. I was looking for her." Opening the back door of the SUV, Ruth waited for Megan to climb in and buckle up.

"Where'd you look?

"I spent the day in Broken Bones."

"Where they found Daddy's body?"

Breathe in. Breathe out. Calm down. "Yes, honey. How did you know that?"

"I heard you talking. Have I ever been to Broken Bones? That's a funny name."

"It is a funny name. It's a funny town. You've never been there, but did you know I lived there for two years?"

"No, did Grandma live there, too?"

"Yes, when I was just a bit older than you."

Megan looked unconvinced. Unfortunately, Ruth knew it had nothing to do with living in Broken Bones and everything to do with Megan trying to imagine her mother as a little girl. Ruth almost laughed. In truth, sometimes Ruth wondered if she'd ever been a little girl.

After Megan buckled herself in the back, Ruth headed for the grocery store, picked up a precooked chicken along with a few side dishes, then headed home. It wouldn't be Megan's usual fare, but it beat fast food. The trip proved unnecessary. When Ruth turned down the street to her house, a little brown Escort waited in the driveway. Carolyn George was home. Without Ruth having to find her and cajole her into feeling wanted and needed, without any fanfare. It didn't bode well.

Megan was out of the car just after Ruth parked. Ruth moved more slowly, trying to decide how to handle just looking at her mother, at a woman who had worked for the Santellises.

The house smelled like hamburger, and Megan ran to hug her grandma in a way Ruth had forgotten. "Mama said you weren't home yet," she exclaimed. "I'm so glad you are."

Hugs shouldn't be awkward, Ruth thought as she followed Megan's example. All the anger-management classes in the world couldn't begin to teach what one five-year-old could in just a matter of minutes. "Mom, you okay?"

"I will be. We're having shepherd's pie for supper."

Ruth nodded, but Megan went in the kitchen baaing like a sheep. Carolyn managed a smile and followed her granddaughter. "I found the recipe online. Looked so good, I thought I'd try it."

Cleaning and cooking had always been Carolyn's way to deal with unhappiness. Well, for the last two years, she'd also been disappearing.

Ruth wearily entered her bedroom and put her backpack and notebooks on the bed. She started to open the one marked George. Pretty soon she'd be asking questions and getting answers she didn't want to hear or know.

"Mama—" Megan ran in the room "—Grandma says it's time to eat. Did you know she put hamburger in the shepherd's pie instead of sheep? I'll bet the sheep are relieved." Just as quickly, Megan exited.

Unbelievably, dinner was fun. Megan somehow managed to miss the feeling of restraint between Ruth and her mother. She kept them entertained with stories about school. Almost before Ruth was ready, dinner was done and Ruth took care of helping Megan with her bath while Grandma did dishes.

It was a night like any other except Ruth's mother was in the kitchen anticipating an unwanted interrogation, and Ruth was helping dry off a little girl who giggled all over, blissfully unaware that her mother was crying inside.

An hour later, after the coloring page homework was complete, the bedtime story read not once but three times and the light turned off, Ruth finally joined her mother in the kitchen, spotless once again now that Mom was home.

She sat with one leg curled under her and the other leg crossed over it. Not bad for a woman heading toward sixty. It was from Carolyn that Ruth got her red hair. Her diminutive size came from Darryl. When Ruth finally got old enough to realize that her dad had been short, she'd wondered if that contributed to the chip he carried on his shoulder. Then she'd learned that in his line of work, the diminutive size was actually a help. He could squeeze through small places, like doggy doors. He could fade into the background, dressed like a teenager, and no one could identify him. And, most of all, he looked too innocent to be a threat. And he was a threat, like the Chihuahua that could take on a Saint Bernard and win.

"So, Mom. We going to talk?"

Carolyn nodded, but didn't say anything.

"Okay, I'll start, what brought you home without me having to hunt you down and beg?"

"I heard you visited the Broken Bones police station. There was a chance—"

"That I'd find out Dad worked for the Santellises."

"And more."

It was the *and more* that sent Ruth scurrying to her bedroom, for two of the notebooks lying on the bed. She grabbed a soda from the fridge and headed back to the table. She curled a leg under her and crossed the other one…then rearranged herself. She didn't give her mother a chance to rethink baring her soul. Ruth started in, ever the master interrogator, "When you disappeared, right after Dustin died, I thought you were having a hard time because I kept bringing up dad, but it was more than that, wasn't it?"

Carolyn nodded her head.

"It was your connection to the Santellises that you were worried about."

Carolyn paled. "I was hoping for a bit more time before I had to tell you."

Ruth felt the table move. It hadn't. Maybe it was the loss of breath she felt, the pain. "Mom, how could you work for that scum?"

"How could I?" It wasn't so much a repeat of the question as a plea for understanding. Ruth had heard the same tone of voice from many a criminal.

And her mom was a criminal. Anyone who'd worked for the Santellises deserved the title.

"How could I?" Carolyn repeated. "We were about to be evicted. I had an eight-year-old, and I had no intention of becoming homeless—"

"So Dad hooked you up with Yano."

"Your father knew nothing about it. Think, Ruth. If Darryl knew I was earning extra money, it would only mean he'd have more to waste. I kept him appeased with what little I made cleaning. The money Yano paid me took care of the extras, such as doctor visits and decent clothes."

"I'd rather you'd have taken the money, saved up and left Dad. We'd have been better off."

"And that's the twenty-thousand-dollar question. Don't think I didn't consider leaving. I did. But you didn't know the Darryl George I married. You only knew the Darryl George he became. I kept thinking I could change him. He'd go back to what he was." Carolyn uncurled her legs. She folded her hands in front of her and leaned forward, looking Ruth right in the eye. "What would you have done, as much as you loved Dustin, if suddenly when Megan was say two years old, he started drinking?"

"One chance. I'd have given him one chance."

"If only life were that simple."

"It is that simple," Ruth said. "There's good and there's evil. Very little in-between."

"I think that's what I regret the most," her mother said sadly. "Somehow, in trying to make the best of a bad situation, I wasn't able to make the best you."

Ruth blinked. "Best me? You're kidding, right? I don't drink. I don't do drugs. I didn't get married because I was pregnant. I—"

"—have no compassion, which is why I have so much trouble telling you just how guilty I am, just how guilty I feel. You'll never forgive me."

Ruth swallowed. It hurt. She took the soda and drank it down in a few fast gulps. Then, she pushed the notebook away. Writing down her mother's words was way too painful. Way too real. Way too honest.

"Oh, Mom." As Ruth said the words, she thought about going to her mother, getting down on her knees and burying her head in her mother's lap, as she'd done so many years ago when she still believed it could all be better. "Mom, I forgive you. You did what you had to do. I'll never understand why you stayed with Dad, but now that I have Megan, I understand why you wanted us to have a home, to have money for the doctor."

"That's not what I need forgiveness for, exactly."

"Exactly," Ruth said slowly, and pursed her lips. Whatever her mother was about to say, couldn't be good and the urge to get next to her mother disappeared. "So, what did you do for Yano Santellis?"

"I worked at the Broken Bones Inn, remember?"

"No."

"I worked while you were in school. People were, are, too trusting. I'd go in their rooms to clean, restock the toilet paper and such. They'd often step outside for a cigarette to give me space. I'd take the car keys they so often left in plain sight, make an impression in clay, and go back to making the bed. It took a second or two. Later,

I'd turn the clay impressions over to the man who ran the Santellis Used-Car Lot."

"Really?"

"Really." Carolyn nodded. "I'd also take their address off the Inn's registry. Then, after a week or a month or so, one of the Santellis or Mallery lackeys would head for the address and steal their car."

"Almost a perfect scenario," Ruth muttered. "If a month had gone by, chances are people wouldn't even remember staying at the motel, let alone mention it."

"Yano gave me a list of the types of cars he wanted. I was always on the lookout. Best money I ever made. You had two Christmases that were decent."

Ruth shook her head. "I don't even remember. Why didn't Yano just teach his goons to hot-wire?"

"He said there was more risk. This way, any witness would say they saw the thief use a key. There'd be time wasted while the cops looked for a family member or friend. Also, sometimes these cars were a day or two away. It gets to be a real pain to hot-wire a car every time you stop for gas or food."

Ruth wasn't sure Yano's reasoning worked, but it must have some credence. Her mother was telling her about a car-thief ring that had been in existence for decades.

"What happened to the cars after they were stolen?"

"They were brought back to Broken Bones."

"To the used-car lot?"

"No, to the scrap yard."

"The one that's been closed for years? The one owned by the Mallerys?"

"Yes, now do you see why I got so scared when Dustin's body was found in the Santellises' shed and the investigating officer was Sheriff Rich Mallery? It's a scenario no one can win. I'm watching you cozy up to a Santellis—"

"I'm not cozying up to Eric," Ruth protested.

"Ruth," Carolyn said. "You were in the car with him today. You're starting to trust him. I can see it in your eyes and hear it in your voice."

"He's not the bad guy, and how did you know we were together today?"

"Benny Mallery called me. He told me to rein you in before you got in trouble."

Benjamin Mallery. He'd seen her at the police station looking at the files of her father and of Yano Santellis. She should have asked for the files on the Mallerys, too, but she guessed they were conveniently missing, *if the Mallerys' misdeeds ever made it to report, that is.* Then, he'd watched her and Eric through his binoculars.

"He knew how to find you when I didn't?"

"I made the mistake of driving up Prospector's Way. I wanted to drive back to the scrap yard, see if it was still there."

"Did you get to the scrap yard?"

"No, the road's a lot bumpier than it used to be. I made it partway and then turned around. I got scared."

"It all makes sense," Ruth said. "Cars disappear all the time in this area. Jose was killed by…"

"Stop!" Carolyn stood up, her cheeks turning red, and her eyes looking frantic. "It's not safe to follow this angle. Leave it alone. Look what happened to Dustin. If something happens to you, where will it leave Megan?"

Sitting back down, Carolyn covered her face with her hands. "I failed you."

"You didn't fail me. I'm strong, Mom. I can handle this."

"That's what Dustin said when I told him."

"What?"

"That morning he'd been talking about two kids he'd arrested and about the cars they were stealing. He was telling me about broken lives. It brought back memories. I—I told him about Benny. I told him where the chop shop was," Carolyn moaned. "The day he disappeared."

EIGHTEEN

Thursday morning it rained, which annoyed Eric to no end because he wanted to spend more time on his laptop and the Internet. He lost electricity at eight and his patience at ten minutes after. He'd been on a roll thanks to his visit to Broken Bones Realty. He'd left there with more questions than he'd gone in with. Exactly what he wanted. More questions definitely led to more answers. And he wanted them all.

He wanted to know about Rich and Benjamin Mallery. The two men, brothers, who'd offered him money for his land. To his way of thinking, first, maybe, they tried to buy the land so that he wouldn't show up and either encroach upon or stumble across whatever they were doing. Hah, maybe they thought he was like his father and wanted to take over. When he did show up, maybe they tried to frame him for the death of Lucille Straus and Dustin Atkins. That would get rid of him, possibly for good.

Questions, questions, questions. What were the Mallerys hiding? Why did they want him gone? Could Benjamin have been working alone? Rich Mallery had maintained a joke of a crime scene that somehow managed to point its finger at Rosa. Funny, according to old articles on the Internet, Sheriff Mallery was actually a pretty decent sheriff.

Of course, everyone thought Jimmy Handley's dad a pretty decent man, too. Yet, he had killed his son.

At first, Eric wasn't sure what else the Mallerys were guilty of besides failing to maintain a crime scene and overzealous use of binoculars. Now, after hours of key words taking him to land-deal sites and property-tax records, he knew Benjamin Mallery was up to something. He, over the past five years, had been buying up land this side of Prospector's Way. Eric and the Winterses were the lone holdouts.

Stretching, Eric glanced at the clock and stood up. He'd been at it since around five, and he'd actually found more than he expected. Thanks to the computer and to Elizabeth Winters's book, which he'd read last night, he'd found out his family, the Santellises, had almost managed to be millionaires *legitimately.*

What had ole Sal Santellis been thinking more than a hundred years ago when he'd sold his share of the Riddell Mine and took off, leaving his family destitute and the Mallerys' fortune secure? Last night, Eric had gone to bed and dreamed about his grandfather, and the cabin, how and why his family managed to hold on to it and nothing else.

This morning, thanks to the Internet, he knew how much his land was worth and how much land in the area was in Benjamin's name, and that Benjamin had paid a pretty penny. Benjamin, who owned a scrap yard and lived in a falling-down cabin.

Eric added the words *Mallery's scrap yard,* yet another of Benjamin's holdings, to his list. Then, he drew a line so it followed the word Mallerys.

Rich Mallery owned a place in town. The sheriff also had a wife and two grown children. Eric had the address and intended to drive by.

After he dressed, climbed in his truck and headed for town, he became uncomfortably aware that what he was feeling bordered on a good mood. He was getting things done: finding out about his family, clearing Rosa's name and helping Ruth.

The same Ruth who drove the SUV that had just turned off Prospector's Way and stopped. She was nuts! Not only was it raining, never good in the Arizona desert where waters pooled aboveground instead of seeping below, but the thunder indicated the potential of a late monsoon storm. She could get stuck in an area where her cell phone and police radio were worthless. Even worse, his morning adventures indicated that Ruth was heading toward Mallery land. Benjamin Mallery's land.

The need to check out Rich Mallery took a backseat to the need to chase down Ruth. Worst-case scenario, stuck in the desert with an irate female who managed to look cute while irritated. Best-case scenario, breakfast with a dumbfounded female who'd somehow taken a wrong turn and appreciated his efforts to point her in the right direction. She was full of surprises.

Now that Ruth knew the truth, the reality of where Dustin's car had been discovered and the proximity of the Mallery junkyard seemed too obvious to miss. She was taking a ridiculous chance coming here without anyone knowing. Oh, her mother might suspect, but Mom was in bed with a sick headache that would only get worse when Sam came over. Tonight, if everything went right, the Mallerys would be behind bars and one of them would tell the truth about Dustin.

Of course, who knew where her mother would be tonight? Sam would do what he could, but Carolyn had withheld information crucial to a murder investigation. Cops frowned on that, even when the person withholding the information was mother-in-law to one cop and mother to another. Thinking about her mother spending the night in jail was more than disconcerting.

This was why what she was doing was so ridiculous. Trespassing just might put her in the cell next to her mother. Or, just as bad, her presence might alert the Mallerys to trouble. Jail was better than death, and with what she knew about the Mallerys now, she knew they wouldn't hesitate to murder her.

But she wanted to make sure her mother's story was plausible, the chop shop still in existence. What if after Dustin's murder they'd moved operation, maybe…

It was the maybe that took her from an ordinary mother dropping her daughter off at school to an extraordinary mother who carried a badge and knew the back roads of Broken Bones, the town that had ruined her life more than once.

She checked the map, one of Dustin's, so far right on target, and started to put her foot on the gas. She almost made it, but Eric Santellis's face appeared in her window.

Funny, she wasn't scared, but somewhat relieved. "What are you doing here?" she asked, after rolling down the window.

"For one, taking an outdoor shower. For two, I saw you and wondered what you were doing." He kept his hands in his pockets and looked reticent, not a natural look for him, but one that melted some of the ice around her heart. "So," he continued, "you going to tell me what you're doing? You're nuts, you know, out here in the rain like this."

"This is close to where they found Dustin's cruiser. My mother's home, she's talking. She said if I follow this road, I'll find a chop shop."

"Your mother told you to come here!"

"She's home, but she didn't exactly send me out here."

He looked at her and waited. Suddenly, she realized how foolish her actions were. The danger she'd put herself in, again. She knew better! Instead of telling him what he wanted to hear, she asked, "Will you come with me?"

"Help, you're asking me for help?"

"Yes." She said it simply, and was surprised by the sudden feeling of security she felt at his nod.

"I will," he said, "and when we're done, I'm taking you to breakfast, and you can tell me about why Doc told you about your mother."

Her mouth opened. She finally closed it and said, "How did you know?"

"I called him."

Annoyed, she muttered, "I've got no privacy anymore. I might as well stand on the corner and yell out my family's secrets."

"Can't be any worse than mine," he said.

"You ever been here before?" She jerked her chin toward the road.

"No. It was on my list of things to do and got moved to first after I saw you turn off the road."

"You have a list?"

"I made it this morning. It's time to figure out who's trying to frame Rosa. You know the Mallerys are involved. I know the Mallerys are involved. It's all leading right to their door, in this case, a scrap-yard entrance."

She felt her mouth open, again. He'd been the constant observer on the porch. It was nice seeing the man of action. "Why is this place on your list?" she repeated.

"Did I tell you that Sheriff Mallery offered to buy my place?"

"No."

"He did, the day Nate found the root cellar. Plus, the day I got out of prison, there was a letter from a Realtor waiting for me."

"An offer to buy your cabin."

"Yes, from a corporation run by Benjamin Mallery. Of course, I didn't know that then. That offer is what inspired me to return to Broken Bones. It inspired me to have the electricity turned on. Still, it took me close to three months to finally move in." He started to reach for his pocket, then he tilted his head upward so that the rain hit him full force. The torrent didn't seem to faze him. "I'd take out my list but then it would get wet and I'd need to rewrite it. Look, you want to ride together or separate?"

"Separate, just in case."

"Just in case what?"

"I don't know, the weather has me spooked."

He looked a little spooked, too. That must be why he gave in so easily. She followed the road for more than a mile, constantly checking to make sure he was still behind her. Her SUV plowed through a running wash with little resistance. Great, the rain meant this would be a quick stakeout. A running wash was nothing to mess with.

A few minutes later she braked to a stop so fast she snapped her neck. She gawked at what was in front of her. Yes, she'd mentally pictured a junkyard. But she hadn't pictured one that resembled a fort made out of bricked cars nor had she prepared for its overwhelming size. It rose in the desert, an atrocity amidst cacti and natural beauty.

She parked her car a good distance away, got out and waited. When Eric finally joined her, she walked closer, counting a column of stacked cars: ten, eleven, thirteen, fifteen… Most stacks were between fifteen and seventeen bricks high. The rain made them look silvery, somewhat blue, and nowhere did Ruth see an entrance. What she saw was a chain-link fence with multiple Keep Out signs.

To a cop, Keep Out meant I Want In. How had she missed this? How had the authorities who investigated Dustin's disappearance missed them? She turned, studying the fortress of pancaked cars. Cars that at one time leaked oil, cushioned families and demanded tune-ups. "I'm here," she said slowly, "because my mother used to help your father steal cars."

"Your mother?"

"Yup, dear old Mom."

Eric started to say something, "Doc left some…" Then, he shook his head, not in denial, but to get rid of some of the water. "Let's get out of the rain."

"No, I want—"

"To get busted?"

"I'll be careful." Ruth took a step, then hesitated. She hated this. This feeling of uncertainty. She'd fought to be strong, stay on top of things, and it bothered her to lose that control in front of Eric. No, that wasn't what was bothering her. What was bothering her was that she expected him to do something.

And he did. He took her by the elbow. "The rain is a blessing in disguise. It might keep the cameras from seeing you."

"What cameras?"

"Those cameras."

Sure enough, perched on each corner of the fortress were cameras, big enough that Ruth should have spotted them the moment she got out of her vehicle, rain or not.

"I can't believe I missed them."

He shrugged. "They're the same colors as the cars."

"You saw them!"

"I just spent the last three years in prison. I'm not likely to miss surveillance cameras."

"I want to go in there, today," she said slowly.

"What's the first thing they teach you at the academy?"

"What?"

"You're a cop. What's the first thing they teach you about entering an unsecured area?"

"Wait for backup," she mumbled.

"Right."

"You can be my backup."

"I agree. I have the aerial view of this scrap yard. Printed it off my computer this morning when I was researching the land the Mallerys own. What you'll see when you get inside are more cars." He stopped, looking at the fortress, unmindful of the water dripping from his chin. He shook his head, amazement taking over his features. "For an out-of-business scrap yard, there's quite a bit of scrap inside. And lots of surveillance."

Ruth looked at the stacks of cars and then back at him. With his hair plastered to his head, he'd ceased looking like a Santellis. He looked like a teenager, an excited teenager.

"What are you thinking?"

"I'm thinking about all the land the Mallerys own. It's quite a chunk, including what you're standing on, and they seem to want more: namely mine. Rich made me an offer. Benjamin made me an offer."

"Oh, my," she said.

"Oh, my." Eric started to say something else, but the rain increased, going from a downpour to a solid sheet. He grabbed her hand, so quickly she almost stumbled.

He didn't need words. She'd lived in Arizona long enough to know they needed to get out of here, should never have risked coming in the first place, not in this rain.

"I'll lead," he shouted as he hurried her to their vehicles. "If I can make it, you probably can, too. Just drive where I drive."

She nodded, her feet catching in the ground as grit and mud and water clung to her shoes. Normally, she loved the rain. It meant less crime, at least in her precinct. Seemed the Gila City criminals didn't much care for getting wet.

Eric opened the door to her SUV and hurried her in. It wasn't until she was behind the wheel and watching him race to his truck that the cold seeped in and set her teeth chattering. She'd been running on pure nerves and now her nerves were shot. Her hands started to shake. To stop them, she gripped the steering wheel and waited for Eric to climb into his truck. He finally did after what seemed too many minutes, then he drove in a circle around her and headed back toward the road. She started the engine and turned around and followed him.

The back of his truck bounced up and down as he traversed puddles and potholes that spelled mishap and danger. She skidded a bit more, but then the back of her vehicle wasn't loaded with trash the way his was. She had nothing to weigh her down. He must have been planning a stop at the local dump. Even in the rain she could make out an old sofa, a ladder, pieces of fencing and a toilet.

He stopped when he came to the wash and that's when she finally realized the predicament they were in. It had been running when she arrived, a gentle flow that barely inspired a rock to move. No more. The wash had risen. But luckily, not that much, *yet.*

Eric exited his truck and went to the edge. He grabbed a stick from the ground and took a cautious step or two into the flow, using the stick to test the ground in front of him. She reached for the door, opened it and started to poke her head out. As if he knew what she was doing, without looking, he held up a hand. He yelled something. Maybe it was Stop or Wait or We're in trouble. Whatever it was, she knew it wasn't good. He walked with the stick a few yards to the left and then a few yards to the right. Finally, he jogged toward her. She closed the door, rolled down the window and immediately felt the pellets of cold rain rush in.

"We going to try it?" She yelled.

"It's fine." Eric looked at her, then at the wash, then back at her. "You drive right where I drive," he ordered.

He started to walk away; she started to roll up the window. But he came back, slowly reached in and squeezed her shoulder. "We can do this."

She nodded, relieved by the tiny word: *we*.

Back at his truck, Eric swung in, hit Reverse and headed to the left. She halfway expected him to gun it and power his way through. He didn't. He took it slowly and carefully, never stopping. The wash was only the size of a one-car driveway. It took him an agonizing minute to cross. He finally drove on dry land and exited the truck. Then, he jumped up and down, whooped and then motioned for her to come across. She started the engine, drove to the exact spot he'd taken off from and cautiously entered the wash. The minute all four tires were submerged, it happened.

She'd heard talk about the walls of water that could careen down a wash, but she'd never seen one. This one hit her and the SUV took on a life of its own. It tilted, down and then up, before turning so she was pointed in the direction of the flow. Then she started to move with the water. Her wheels weren't touching land.

This was not good.

Not good at all.

NINETEEN

Before Eric had time to react, yet another wall of water careened down the wash. Had two washes combined as one? People lost their lives in running washes! And no matter how fast Eric's feet moved, he couldn't get to Ruth fast enough.

Then, as if God had heard an unspoken prayer, the SUV stopped. Not completely. No, Eric couldn't be that lucky. But, the SUV was certainly stuck on something.

Ruth was moving inside the vehicle. He could see her undoing her seat belt, grabbing her backpack and rolling down the window. Great, he was more panicked than she was. She was doing something more constructive than panicking. Carefully, she pulled herself from the window and climbed on top of the SUV. It chose that moment to slide a bit. She hit the top of the cab, feet spread-eagled in front of her, then another bump sent her rolling until she was sprawled on her stomach on the hood, facing the water.

The SUV stopped moving again. This time it pointed toward the side of the wash where Eric stood. He could almost catch her if she jumped. No, she'd send the SUV moving again trying to get traction. He glanced up and down the wash, looking for something to hold on to. He was more than willing to get in the water, but he had to have something to help him make it to dry land once he had her.

Maybe he could drive his truck in the water—it was heavy—and she could walk across using his truck as a bridge. But if the truck got stuck, they'd both be stuck, and he could see her hands shaking. She was drenched, cold, shivering.

Maybe he could find something… Glancing at the truck, he saw it. The old ladder was missing two rungs, but maybe it could perform one more duty before retirement. He started for his truck, yelling back at Ruth. "Hold on!"

He knew she couldn't hear him, yet she glanced up, nodded and scrambled until she was sitting with her back against the windshield, her backpack clutched to her side.

The ladder wasn't that heavy, but it was wet, and cold, and his fingers felt stiff. Finally, he arrived back where her SUV was and carefully placed the ladder so it was up against the bumper and then firmly gripped in the dirt at his feet. The SUV moved a bit, but as if God had a finger pressing on its hood, it stopped just long enough for Ruth to crawl off the hood and onto the ladder.

She immediately spilled into the water. The current too strong to allow her the type of footing she needed to walk across. She held on and pulled herself a step or two toward dry land. Eric tightened his grip, just as the ladder slipped off the bumper and Ruth played a momentary game of crack the whip with Eric at the head and the ladder acting as the whip.

Eric watched one of her hands slip. He fought the urge to jump in the water, save her, and instead did the sensible thing. He applied all his strength to keep his grip on the ladder. Ruth flopped in the water trying to get her balance while fighting her way back to the ladder with her other hand. The ladder swayed and Ruth's body went with it, close to land. Eric risked it all. He plunged into the wash, grabbed her and flung her toward land.

And he lost his footing and went under.

Surprise opened his mouth. The taste of cold water, sand and surprise closed his mouth. Then, he was back up and crawling toward Ruth. He collapsed at her feet, exhausted yet exhilarated. What a ride. It had been a long time since he'd felt so alive. He looked at her, sitting there in the mud, and he wanted nothing more than to take her in his arms and celebrate life.

Instead, he jumped up and offered her a hand. "We need to get dry clothes."

She flipped her hair out of her eyes, hair that resembled tangled, dark seaweed, and looked at him. "Boy, do we ever." And, to Eric's surprise, she took his hand and started laughing.

He pulled her to her feet and waited a moment, to see if she was about to lose it or if she was really laughing.

She hadn't lost it. Instead, she said, "Oh, my. That was close. You know how many wash rescues I've been involved in? Ten. Ten. I've kept count. And each and every time I told the driver how much of an idiot they were. Each and every time I told them they deserved to lose their vehicle." She looked at her SUV. Now, obediently, it stayed in one position, barely swaying, almost looking apologetic. "I deserved that. I should have realized your truck was heavier. I should have hopped in with you. I'm an idiot."

He had no answer. He was afraid that speaking would break the spell.

The spell that still had her hand in his.

The cab of his truck proved that this was a man who used his vehicle. He had tools, hats, old receipts, so much clutter that it took her a few minutes just to rearrange the old fast-food restaurant bags so she, and her very wet backpack, could squeeze in. He quickly started to stuff trash behind the seat. "I can't seem to get enough."

"Huh?"

"Fast foods," he said. "The day I got out of jail, I had a cheeseburger, fries and a shake. Now, every time I go to Wickenburg, it's my first stop."

"You can always throw away the empty bags and ketchup containers."

"I do, eventually."

When she was finally settled, he started the truck and turned on the heat. After cool air blew for ten minutes, he shut it off. "I've never needed it before. I had no idea it didn't work," he apologized. "Where do you want to go? My house is the closest. We can get some dry clothes. Or do you want to head to town?"

Ruth looked at her watch. It had fared better than her body and clothes. Dirt clung to her hands, and they were a ghastly white—made more apparent by their shaking. She'd never been so cold. Still, she said, "Town. It's already past noon. I can buy some clothes at the secondhand store and get back to Gila City in time to pick Megan up."

"Call your mother."

"If I have to, I will, but I'd rather not."

"Why?"

"She's in bed with a headache." She thought he might ask for more information, but he didn't. Instead, he concentrated on the road. The rain made driving nearly impossible. She reached for her backpack, grimacing at how wet it was, and already aware of what she'd pulled out. Sodden notebooks, ink running, three years worth of notes down the drain, literally. The loss of her notebooks saddened her more than the loss of her vehicle. But now was not the time to throw a tantrum. She was much too cold. Trying to make the best of a bad situation, Ruth turned her attention to Eric and watched as he swerved to the side of the road to avoid the good-sized puddles that his truck might not make it through. For an old truck, Eric's vehicle didn't seem to mind the rough terrain. Her SUV would have been skidding and shaking. Eric's truck wasn't skidding, and the only shaking going on was hers.

"I'm going as fast as I dare," Eric said.

Her teeth started to chatter. "I know."

For the next few miles, they drove in silence—him concentrating on the road, and her concentrating on him. Finally, to take her mind off how miserable she was, both inside and out, she said, "My mother has a headache because we're meeting with Sam Packard tonight before church."

"That would give me a headache, too."

If he'd said anything else, she might have stopped there, but instead of curiosity, pressing questions, or, even worse, sympathy, he offered compassion. That word again. *Compassion.* She didn't have any, but apparently Eric did.

She told him everything. The words spilling from her like the water that rushed down the wash and destroyed both her SUV and her notebooks. She told about her father and the kind of life they lived. About her mother, who turned out to have secrets Ruth never dreamed of. She told him about Dustin and their hopes, their dreams. She finished by telling him about tonight's meeting.

"I'm picking Megan up and taking her to a friend's house. Then, Mom and I are meeting Mitch and Sam at a restaurant."

"Rosa said that's what you did last time."

"Rosa said?"

"When she was spilling her guts about her secrets. She said Sam arranged a meeting at a restaurant. You were there, right?"

"I was. And, you're right. This is much the same." She looked at him. "Rosa sure surprised us with her secret. I'm betting there are things my mother didn't tell me last night. Things that might bring your family into the spotlight again."

He laughed, and it was a mirthful sound, much like her laugh. "My family is seldom far from the spotlight."

"They are now," she insisted. "Until you found Dustin, it probably had been a good month since the name Santellis appeared in the paper."

"A good month, indeed," he agreed.

"I wonder if Rosa will be at the meeting tonight, too." The words came out before she could stop them. Musing aloud was dangerous; every cop knew that. And, she was musing in front of a Santellis. A Santellis who had just saved her life, *and more.*

"If I know Rosa," Eric said, "she'll be there."

"She's very up-front. From that first meeting, when Sam first arrested her over a year ago, I could tell she'd be a good cop." What had surprised Ruth was Rosa's ability to be a good friend. One who Ruth missed. Now the only time Ruth saw Rosa was at church. Gone were the uplifting phone calls, the occasional coffee in the morning, the girls' night out opportunities.

"She was a good nurse," Eric said.

"I never saw that side of her."

"She had a problem with the ethics board after she helped bust the drug ring. Seems patient confidentiality is more important than getting drug dealers off the street. She lost that career."

Ruth looked out the window. "Sometimes we sacrifice the wrong things. But Rosa's a good cop now. She found a new path."

Eric nodded. "You feel like you're sacrificing your mother, don't you?"

"Yes."

"It's probably been hard for her all these years, carrying such a secret, especially once people she knew and loved started to die."

"My husband," Ruth whispered.

"Just think of how free she'll feel when she comes clean. She'll know she helped keep someone else alive." Eric slowed down and looked at Ruth.

It was an honest look, a straightforward look, a look that held a promise she didn't know how to accept.

He kept talking. "Maybe the person she's helping to keep alive is you."

Ruth shook her head. "I don't know. I sort of wish she'd tell me everything. Then, I'd send Mom away, so far they'd never find her."

"You'd be willing to do that? Lose contact with your mother? Possibly lose your career?"

"I just want my life back."

"Sending your mother away, not letting her face the truth, is not getting your life back."

Ruth stared out the truck's window. He was right about that. She could never get her life back, not the life she wanted anyway.

"Sometimes you have to make a sacrifice to get things in order. I did. I sacrificed three years. It kept my brothers from going after Rosa. It kept her safe. I'm a better person because of the sacrifice I made. I can live with myself."

"She wasn't safe, she was hunted. And until you found those bodies in your shed, you were trying to live *by yourself.* That's never healthy."

"Rosa's alive today. That's what counts."

One thing for sure, this was the most sensible Santellis she'd ever met. Both sensible and compassionate.

"Sam's bringing Mitch Williams with him tonight, from internal affairs. Sam called him because of Rich Mallery being a sheriff."

"I know Mr. Williams. He's very good at what he does. He's also not the most merciful. Why didn't you ask for someone else? You know how he treated Rosa. He didn't want to offer her a deal at all."

"Not at first he didn't, but he came around. I asked for him because while Sam and Rosa were in hot pursuit, Mitch and I were working behind the scenes—together. I got to know him, and I trust him."

"I guess I understand. I trusted Jimmy with my life. He was as driven as Williams. I trust Rosa with my life, still do, and I'll do anything to save hers. Friends—" his voice tapered off "—and family *are* life. Maybe that's why I needed to be alone and regroup. I seem to be running short on both."

Unfortunately, she knew exactly what he was talking about. His family was pretty much gone. Rosa and Sam were probably his only friends, and Rosa was in trouble. The cold was starting to get to her, either that or she was going soft. The words almost hurt, but still she had to get them out. "I never thought I'd say this, but I'm sorry about your older brothers. The way they died and that their killer was never caught."

"Yeah, well, coming from you that's really something. This also must mean you no longer think my family had anything to do with Dustin's death."

"It's really looking that way." What she didn't say was how relieved she was to think she was wrong.

"Well, don't go getting all sappy on me. We don't know for sure you're wrong. After all, my brothers were still alive and kicking when Dustin took his last breath."

"But—"

"Don't go soft on my brothers just because you're getting to know me. They were both killers."

Getting to know me.

She heard the words and knew what they meant. She'd recognized the fit back at his cabin the first day when she sat on his couch and he knew enough to sit across the room on the floor, just to give her space right when she needed it. Then, he'd paid attention to her notebooks, asking questions and providing insight. Not even Sam had appreciated how much time she invested in her scribing.

Oh, what a tangled web we weave, she thought. No way would a Santellis and a cop make a good match. Not even an honest Santellis and an honest cop.

Then, she heard his next words.

"But I still miss them."

She started to reach across the fast-food bags, the tools, the trash and all; she wanted to touch him, to offer condolences, maybe offer that compassion her mother so wished for, but his eyes met hers and she stopped.

The look was enough.

And suddenly, she wasn't so cold.

They finally reached Prospector's Way, and he stopped, looking both ways, squinting to see through the rain. "You didn't know them before my old man corrupted them. I still remember when Tony thought he'd be a professional baseball player. I remember when Sardi wanted to work at a zoo."

Ruth couldn't breath. She couldn't swallow. It was almost word for word what her mother had said about her father. *You didn't know him back when...*

The truck lurched as Eric started to turn.

That's when a loud ping sounded, then another, yet one more, and the truck heaved to one side. It all happened so quickly that by the time Eric grabbed Ruth, pushed her head down, the shots had stopped.

His heart had stopped! Stopped! And all because someone he cared about was in danger.

"He got your tire!" Ruth said, going for her seat belt. She had no idea how scared he was.

Eric reached across and stopped her. "You're not getting out."

"But—"

"But," he echoed, "the shooter probably has a bead on this truck and you."

TWENTY

He'd driven with a flat before. He'd also driven in bad rainstorms. He'd just never driven in bad rain on just a rim with someone shooting at him. He headed down the hill and toward town, bright lights and crowds.

The side of the truck with the flat got caught in a mire of mud. It spun a moment, going nowhere, Eric rocked the truck forward and backward and got lucky. The truck actually moved. Bad enough to be dealing with rough terrain, but the addition of mud, potholes and a lopsided truck made the going slow. Not a good speed when someone with a gun was behind you. Even if the gunfire had stopped.

Ruth had resnapped her seat belt and now hunched down and stared out the window. She was no longer shivering. She'd taken a gun from her backpack and held it protectively.

"Do you think they're pursuing?" she asked.

"No, I think they stopped."

The truck bumped along for a few minutes, with Ruth still ducked down and staring out the window. Finally, she sat up and stared at Eric. "Benjamin Mallery?" she asked.

"Probably."

"He owns a gun."

"Probably more than one."

"Why did he stop shooting?" Ruth looked incredulous.

"He did what he wanted to do. He let us know we were unwelcome."

"He didn't do what he wanted to do," Ruth argued. "We're still alive."

Eric shook his head. "He wasn't trying to kill us."

"I think he was."

"We weren't expecting gunfire. We were sitting ducks. If he'd wanted to kill us, we'd be dead."

Ruth glanced at her watch and frowned. Eric glanced at his. It was almost two. At the rate they were going, it would be close to five before they reached town. Almost another hour before they could get to Gila City. "What time is your meeting?"

"Five."

"You're never going to make it."

"I'm more bothered by the fact I won't make it to pick up Megan." She dug her cell phone out and flipped it open. "There's either no service or thanks to a soaking I no longer own a working phone. You sure you can't go any faster?"

"I'm sure." What he didn't tell her was how lucky the five miles per hour was. The rain had slacked off a bit—*bit* being the defining word. Right now, the rain was going down the windshield instead of up. If they hit the wrong patch of mud, they'd stop moving, and no amount of rocking would free them. He reached on top of the dash and retrieved his cell phone. "Try mine."

A minute later she said, "Well, at least yours says *No Service*. That's more than mine did." She turned in the seat, looking out the window. "I can't see a thing."

"Our shooter could, remember that. We're lucky he just wanted to scare us."

She nodded. "I know just how lucky I am. I'll miss my meeting, but I'll get to tuck Megan into bed tonight. I'm alive."

"We're alive," he said softly.

The words were loaded, and Ruth understood. She picked at her shirt and stared out the window. The truck bumped slowly along, giving Ruth plenty of time to study the terrain and think.

All this time she'd blamed the Santellis brothers for Dustin's death. No one had considered the Mallerys. Maybe if they had, the scrap yard would have been searched years ago. Maybe if they had, John, the mayor, might have mentioned the land his family owned. She hadn't known he owned the Last Chance Café. How did he live with himself? He used Stop Crime as a political platform. No wonder the number of cars stolen in the area was still an issue.

She knew Rich Mallery, as well. Broken Bones and Gila City were within throwing distance of each other. They'd met up in court a few times, been to a few of the same parties. Ironically, Dustin had liked the man. She hadn't disliked him. Until he took over her husband's crime scene and messed things up. Looked as though he was covering his own trail. He'd have succeeded, too, if not for Sam and Rosa bringing in Nate, if not for her mother finally talking, if not for Eric. She had been so sure the Santellises were guilty; she'd have played right into Mallery's hand.

Life certainly was strange.

But not as strange as the looks she received when Eric finally reached the outskirts of Broken Bones in his muddy and broken-down truck. He pulled into the parking lot of Axel's Bar. "No, I'm not going in for a drink," he responded to her look. "Wait here. I won't be long."

Wait here. I won't be long. Words her father had spoken a few times. But, with Eric, she believed them. He came out ten minutes later and opened her door, motioning for her to exit. "You ready?" he asked.

"For what?"

"To head for Gila City."

"What did you do inside the bar? We need to contact the police and—"

"And that's exactly what we'll do. But not from here. You're forgetting the law is a Mallery here. We have no idea how loyal his two deputies are. Plus, you have that nice little meeting with Mitch Williams tonight. Who better to tell?"

Yup, he was the sensible Santellis. She checked her watch again. She already knew the time. She'd checked five minutes ago. She'd checked four minutes ago. The meeting he referred to had started almost an hour ago.

"I've borrowed us a vehicle, legally. I paid two hundred dollars. Inside that bar, there's a very happy man who, indeed, recognized the name Santellis. We have it until tomorrow night, this time. Let's not waste daylight."

She stepped from the truck. The cold immediately swept around her, causing her to pause a moment before she held up a hand to cease Eric's talking. "Don't tell me what you did or said to get this vehicle. It's best if I don't know." The rain had settled down to a light mist, but it didn't matter. Her clothes were so saturated she almost felt as though she was wearing body armor.

Ruth circled the truck, slowly, looking for the shots. Eric's truck had seen better days even before taking the bullets.

"You find what you're looking for?" Eric asked.

"I only found two of the bullet holes."

"Are you counting the tire?"

Ruth looked at the mud-laden flat. "Hmm, I wasn't even thinking of that one."

"Well, come on, we've got a few other things to do." Eric led her to a red Mustang. Well, at least the hood was red. Both doors were blue, and the body was primer gray. Color really didn't matter. What the Mustang did have was four good tires. Once they settled in, Eric drove half a block and stopped at a secondhand store. "Come on."

She didn't need to hear the invitation twice. This particular secondhand store had been in existence back when she was a child. Her mother shopped here. A few minutes later, and after Eric gave the woman an extra twenty, a tired-looking cashier gave permission for them to change clothes in the bathrooms. The jeans Ruth put on were well-worn in the knees, a bit flared at the bottom and tighter than she'd go with if she wasn't in such a hurry to get home. The shirt was a striped red-and-white pullover.

It smelled.

The socks were perfect and the shoes fit. She grabbed the sweater Eric had forced on her, gathered her old wet and filthy clothes and hurried out to meet Eric.

He managed, even in hand-me-downs, to look perfect.

"Where are your old clothes?"

"I tossed them."

Spoken like the son of a wealthy man. Ruth felt a momentary jolt of recognition. Yup, a Santellis wouldn't think twice about discarding perfectly good clothes. She, on the other hand, asked the cashier for a bag, stuffed her clothes in it and started for the car.

He followed, held the passenger-side door open for her and slid in. Before he started the car, he handed over his phone. "Call who you need to."

Her mother's cell phone was turned off. So was Sam's. She had Mitch's number, but not memorized. It was stored on her cell phone. She called the Gila City Police Station, repeated the number out loud three times and in a few minutes was dialing Mitch. His cell phone wasn't turned off. No surprise. Mitch answered in just thirty seconds. Ruth could hear restaurant sounds in the background. She could hear voices, not her mother's, but both Sam's and Rosa's. There was even a bit of laughter.

"Where are you? We're worried." Mitch sounded more annoyed than worried.

"I'm in Broken Bones. It's a long story, but I need you to pick up Benjamin Mallery. He shot at us, about three hours ago. We were leaving his scrap yard."

His pause told her more than words.

"Mitch, why aren't you surprised?"

What she heard next was muzzled conversation, between Mitch and Sam. Rosa chimed in and so did Ruth's mother. Ah, so she was there. Ruth gritted her teeth and said in an aside to Eric. "I need to be there."

"I'll hurry," Eric said.

Mitch came back on the line. "Ruth, if Benny shot at

you, then we're surprised. We've had him under surveillance for a week and a half. He disappeared three days ago. Even his brother Rich thinks he's dead."

"Dead?"

"So it wasn't Benjamin?" she whispered.

"We've had him under investigation ever since Nate figured out the sheriff was deliberately trying to destroy a crime scene."

TWENTY-ONE

Eric seemed to be patiently concentrating on the road as Ruth finished her conversation with Mitch. She hung up and waited, but he was silent as the miles and daylight disappeared. Gila City was just a half hour ahead. Strange. Ruth expected all kinds of questions. She waited awhile, to see if he'd talk first. He didn't.

"What's wrong?" she finally asked. The moment the words were out, she wanted them back. The real question, the true question, was *"What wasn't wrong?"*

"I'm mad at myself. I assumed it was Benjamin Mallery. Yet, I knew that he had a high-powered rifle. I saw it the other day when we drove by on our way to the Winterses'. Rifle shots don't ping. I should have realized we were being shot at by a revolver."

"You know enough to tell a rifle from a revolver?"

He gave her a look that chilled her. "What's my last name?" he said.

"Oh."

"Oh, yes. I've got quite a lot to live up to. When I left prison, one of the guards, a Christian no less, gave me a piece of advice. He told me to legally change my last name. And I thought about it. See, I knew where he was coming from. There's a reason why parents name their kids Matthew, Paul and Mary. It's the same reason why parents don't name their kids Satan, Judas or Jezebel. To his way of thinking, who'd want the name Santellis?"

"So why didn't you take his advice?"

"Changing a last name is a lot more complicated than changing a first. There was a time when the name Santellis meant something. There are still Santellises in Southern Italy who are blissfully unaware of what the American Santellises have done to sully the name."

"I changed my name," Ruth said. "I was so glad when I married Dustin and could take his last name. I almost wish my mother would get remarried."

"I'm proud of my name," Eric said. "I'm just not proud of my family."

Ruth was once again reminded of her mother's words. *Somehow, in trying to make the best of a bad situation, I wasn't able to make the best you. You have no compassion.*

"Someday," Eric continued, "my little brother or my sister may need the help of a Santellis, an upstanding Santellis. Someday my nephews need to know that there's more to the Santellis name than blood and bullets."

The first few buildings of Gila City came into sight. Ruth sat up. "We were meeting at The Fifties Diner. They have a corner booth away from the rest of the customers. It's almost seven. I can't imagine they're still there."

They weren't. The corner booth already hosted a family busy devouring ice cream and pie. The bunch looked as if they didn't have a care in the world. Ruth envied them.

"Let me use your cell phone."

Eric handed it over, and Ruth dialed her mother's number. Still no answer. Ruth shook her head. "Mom had to have picked up Megan from school. Then, because she had the meeting, she probably took Megan to a friend's."

They tried Ruth's house first. Carolyn's car wasn't parked in the driveway.

"Where do want to try next?" Eric asked. "You want to call Sam or Rosa since your mom is not answering?"

Ruth checked her watch. "It's after seven. They're at church. That's it! It's Wednesday night. Mom took Megan to church."

Eric looked taken aback. "You mean, your mother would give testimony that might put her away for life and then go to church?"

Ruth almost laughed at the thought. "It won't surprise me to find Mom sitting in a car in the church's parking lot. This is Megan's doing. Life might be spiraling out of control for Mom and me, but Megan's life is still pretty much the same. And the same means going to church on Wednesday night. She loves class. For weeks, they've been making a Noah's ark out of cardboard. The thing is huge."

Eric nodded. "In length, Noah's ark stretches about two football fields."

"How do you know these things?"

"I did a lot of reading in prison. As for literature, the Bible can't be beat. I mean, think about it. It's a collection of writings of the world's earliest history."

"Then, you believe the Bible."

Eric's face shut down. "I believe the history."

It was not the time or place to probe deeper. "Let's

go," she urged. "I need to see my mother, and I want to check on Megan."

The church was only three blocks away. Mom's car was parked near the back. It was empty. Ruth whispered, "Unbelievable. I think she's inside."

"Maybe she's feeling redeemed in more ways than one," Eric said.

Ruth slammed the door and considered. She'd invited her mother every single week for the last few months, and look, Carolyn finally attended, on her own initiative. "You coming?"

Eric shook his head. "I'll wait in the car."

"It might be a while. Maybe you should head back home. I'll ride home with my mother."

"No, I want to hear what happened with your mom and Mitch Williams."

"Then, come in."

"You're not thinking, Ruth. What are people going to say if you walk into church with a Santellis?"

That stopped her. Tongues would wag. Hers certainly had back when she thought him a criminal.

She didn't think that anymore.

"What if I told you I didn't care?"

"I'd tell you that *I care*. You go on in. I'll be here when you get out."

Ruth looked at the church. Dusk cast a dark shadow over the building. Rain still dripped tears down the gutters and trees. The Bible mentioned rain. God had sent it to the earth in Genesis. It had wiped away the wickedness of man and left just the righteous.

Today, she'd almost drowned, she'd been shot at, and God had watched over her every minute.

Light spilled from the windows of the church and the voices of the saved carried on the breeze. Those inside were singing, and they were singing one of the few songs Ruth knew the words to. "Amazing Grace."

The same God who had watched over her this day had also watched over Eric Santellis and had probably sent Eric Santellis to the scrap yard to keep Ruth safe. Walking to the driver's side, she opened the door and stated, "You're coming in."

"That an invitation?" he asked wryly.

"No," she said bluntly. "I don't have much luck with invitations, whether I'm getting them or giving them, so consider it an order."

As Eric walked toward the doors, he tried to remember the last time he'd stepped inside a church. Maybe his mother's funeral. He'd been fifteen years old. His older brothers had flanked their father. Eric, Mary and Kenny had sat to the side. Mary had cried during the whole service, and Eric held her hand. He'd wanted to cry, but he felt caught—caught between childhood and adulthood. If he cried, his father might forget he existed. If he didn't cry, his father might notice and start asking things of him. He hadn't cried, and his father hadn't asked anything of him. It was as if his mother's death had given the three youngest children an escape, one that Eric wanted, and one that Kenny didn't.

"Come on." Ruth reached out to him.

All it took to lead him into church was a small and soft hand. She led him as if he were a sheep going to slaughter, and he felt just as vulnerable.

The inside of the church looked nothing like the church

of his youth. It was much smaller and had no stained glass. Ruth took off down a hallway, dragging him with her. About five doors down, she stopped and peered through a window. He watched as she waved. Her whole body relaxed. She moved aside.

"My little girl is the one with two ponytails. She's wearing the red shirt."

He looked through the glass. Inside was a table with about eight chairs. All empty. About six children were sprawled on the floor on a piece of blue paper. Fish decorated the paper, along with starfish and waves. Two children worked on the ark. The little girl with the red shirt was sitting with a dark-haired little boy. They were making paper elephants. Eric tried to remember. Should the children make two elephants or seven?

"That teacher must be a saint," Eric finally said.

"No, we're all sinners." Ruth blushed after she said the words. "That's what Sam and Rosa keep telling me." Then, she tugged on his sleeve. "Let's go find my mother."

Carolyn sat with Sam and Rosa near the back of a classroom. She looked uncomfortable. Then she saw Ruth and relief spread across her face, until she saw Eric.

Rosa, on the other hand, glowed. She mouthed *"Eric"* and accompanied it with a huge grin. Sam managed to look pleased, too. Okay, maybe this next hour would be manageable. A few members of the class smiled. They obviously didn't know who he was. A few visibly shrank.

Ruth scooted around the first two rows of people, took a folding chair from against the wall and crowded next to her mother before sitting down. Eric followed her example.

Then, the woman sitting beside Eric handed him a

Bible and whispered, "We're in the eighth chapter of Acts." And like that the storm in Eric's heart stopped blowing.

The teacher didn't pause, just continued with his lesson. Eric remembered him. The preacher, the one who'd come out the day they found the body, the one who didn't know about his family.

The lesson was about prayer. How ironic. Eric had thought about praying that very morning when Ruth went in the water. Thinking about saying a prayer and attending church all on the same day.

Around him, members of the class shuffled the pages of their Bibles. Sam and Rosa shared one. Ruth's mother probably didn't own one. Eric had given his to a fellow prisoner. He'd figured the guy needed it more than he did.

Ruth's Bible was probably at the end of the wash right now, in much the same shape as her notebooks.

A few people spoke up during class. Most stared at Eric, but no one left. Finally, Bibles shut and it seemed that people relaxed. Ah, lesson over. Steve Dawson stepped away from the podium, a bit more personal now. "Friends," he said, "we have a special visitor tonight."

If it weren't for the two rows of people he'd have to leap over, Eric would already be out the door.

"I first met Eric Santellis—" lightning did not strike the man dead for saying Eric's name in church "—when our own Ruth finally found out what happened to her husband. Even in the worst of situations, he opened his home—"

As if there was a choice.

"—and he's opened up his home every day since.

"I started praying for Eric when I realized the burden

he carried because of his name. Folks, remember, according to Matthew 'If you love those who love you, what reward will you get.' Please welcome Eric Santellis. You'll soon see the reward in knowing him."

Rosa nodded vigorously.

And to Eric's amazement, Ruth did, too.

Every head turned to stare at Eric. The majority of the Wednesday-night class was female, over sixty and wearing blue. They smiled. It was the people near his own age who seemed more hesitant. Until Ruth reached over and took his hand. "He saved my life today," she announced, and proceeded to tell about the wash.

Suddenly, welcome oozed from the room. All Eric needed to do was smile back and acceptance was his.

TWENTY-TWO

Ruth finished her shake, hamburger and fries. Then, she finished Megan's fries. Then, she started stealing fries from her mother. She couldn't remember ever being this hungry before. Eric didn't eat much. Ruth could have cheerfully snatched food from him. Maybe she would have, if they'd been alone.

Sam was outside talking on his cell phone. Ruth considered eyeing his food but a pregnant Rosa already was doing the *what's mine is mine and what's yours is mine* routine.

Because Megan was with them, they'd chosen a fast-food joint with an attached playground. It was a wise choice. It kept Megan occupied, but she knew something was going on. She'd go play and then come back, as if worried the dreaded something would happen without her. Because of her, conversation was guarded. There were indirect references to the gunshots, the incident in the wash, namely what was Ruth thinking and how could she be so calm after losing her SUV and after being shot at?

Ruth was somewhat leery to admit she mourned her

notebooks more than her vehicle. Not a sensible choice for a single mother with a single paycheck.

Sam finally walked back in, took one look at the two cold fries and piece of hamburger bun awaiting his return, and went back to the counter to order more food.

When he returned, he sat down and bowed his head in silent prayer. It still gave Ruth pause to watch this man, her onetime partner, go to the Lord in thanks. It made her think; it made her want something, perhaps whatever peace he had.

Megan popped over, gave him a quick hug and took a drink of her shake. "We ready to go, Mom?"

"Not yet, Megan. Soon."

Sam waited until Megan was inside the tube slide before saying, "Mitch is about ten minutes away. He's bringing Nate with him. They've been at Axel's Bar's parking lot looking at those bullet holes on your truck, Eric."

"Do they know where Benjamin is now?" Eric leaned forward.

"Not that I know of." Before Sam could say any more, Nate and Mitch walked in. Nate stepped up to the counter, ordered two cups of coffee, and after handing one to Mitch, they joined everyone else.

When Mitch Williams sat at the next table, Ruth felt Eric's body tense. He was so close to her she felt his warmth and considering how cold she'd been most of the day— thanks to a summer monsoon—the warmth was appreciated.

"We looked at the bullet holes," Mitch started. "They look like they came from a standard revolver."

"Albeit an old one." Nate added, "We know direction of fire and bullet caliber. They're also really unusual. Sorta shaped like keyholes."

"I've never seen anything like it," Mitch said.

Nate smiled. "It's homemade."

"The sheriff?" Ruth asked. "Lots of police officials collect old guns."

"He's not your shooter," Mitch said.

"Nope," Nate spoke up. "Of all things, he was busy rescuing a mother and her two kids. They got caught up in a wash located a few miles east of yours, right before yours erupted. They lost their vehicle, too."

"He's in Gila City right now answering quite a few questions," Mitch said.

"Is he—" Ruth started.

"Involved?" Mitch's frown deepened. "No and yes. He's not part of the ring. In all ways but one, he's an honest cop. He knew his brother operated a chop shop, and up until five years ago, he thought it was about to end."

Mitch turned to Eric. "Seems Benjamin was in cahoots with first your father and then your brother-in-law, Eddie."

Eric didn't look surprised; he also didn't answer.

"Eric?" Ruth said softly, and nudged his knee with hers. It worked.

"Eddie was in charge of the used-car lot. My father thought maybe it was the one place he couldn't mess up."

"Your father might have been right," Nate said. "Up until about five years ago, during Eddie's regime, the chop shop only dealt with cars taken from out of state."

"Good business," Ruth's mother whispered, just loud enough for them to hear. "Yano said not to pollute your own backyard. What happened a few years ago to change that way of thinking?"

"Eddie was in and out of prison so often that Dad took

the business away from him," Eric said. "He gave it to my sister Mary, but she didn't do anything with it."

"Thus the 'Going Out of Business' that never happened," Mitch said. "We always wondered why the Closed sign went up and the Open sign never appeared."

"Dad was getting sick, and Tony thought the chop shop was chump change."

"You know a lot about your father's business." Mitch busied himself brushing imaginary crumbs off the table. The statement was meant to sound offhand, but Ruth knew it was calculated.

Eric didn't even blink. "All that happened about the time I first started helping Jimmy. I made sure I knew what was happening with my family." It was the right thing to say. Mitch had the decency to look remorseful.

"You'll relate to this, Eric," Nate said. "Seems the sheriff's only crime was an unwillingness to turn on his brother."

"Rich swears he doesn't know who Benny's working with. He thinks whoever it is carried Dustin to your shed. At first he thought Benjamin responsible. It about killed him thinking his brother a murderer. See, he blamed Dustin's disappearance on the Santellises, too." Nate looked at Ruth. "When Lucille Straus's body turned up, he started worrying about Benny's involvement. But now he says Benny had no clue the bodies were there or how they got there."

Mitch added, "Rich is resigning. He's having trouble living with himself. Tampering with a crime scene went against his grain, especially now that he knows you two were shot at today."

"Then why did he do it?" Ruth asked.

"He loves his brother," Eric said.

Ruth's mother spoke up. "Rich pretty much raised Benny after their parents died. It wasn't always easy. I think he became a cop because of all the trouble Benny got into. He couldn't help Benny, but maybe he would help others."

Nate started gathering trash. "Because of those shots fired today, we figure that Dustin's killer is close and feeling desperate. He's making mistakes. Like using the same gun to shoot at you as he used to shoot and kill both Dustin and Lucy."

"And desperate people take dangerous chances." Mitch looked at his watch. "Look, let's continue this conversation in the morning. I still need to chase down a few leads tonight, and quite frankly—" he looked at Ruth "—you look about ready to collapse."

"Megan already has," Rosa said softly.

Of all people, Megan had chosen Eric to collapse against. He didn't look as if he minded. Ruth tried to shake away the fatigue. It dulled her senses, caused her to miss the obvious. When had Megan joined them? How much had she heard?

"Have I put Megan in danger?" Ruth looked at Mitch.

"We're not exactly sure. Just in case, we're posting a guard at your house."

"Good," Ruth said.

Mitch turned to Eric. "And you can't go back to your cabin."

"I'll be fine. I—"

"It has nothing to do with trust or police procedure. The road's underwater. You'd need a boat to get home."

"You'll stay with us," Rosa said.

"Don't even try to argue with her," Sam said. "Pregnant women win every argument, every time."

"That's right. Argue with me and I just might have an unexpected pain." Rosa patted her stomach.

"Desperate people take dangerous chances," Eric reminded. "I don't want to be at your house when that happens."

"Whoever it is cannot possibly know you're at our house. Personally—" Rosa looked at Ruth "—I wish you'd all come to our house."

"There's safety in numbers," Sam agreed.

"I'm the guard," Nate said, ending the debate. "I'll be watching her house."

Eric had gone without sleep before. He just couldn't ever remember being so bothered about tossing and turning. Every fiber of his being wanted to be somewhere else. He didn't necessarily want to be home: nothing there. In all honesty, he wanted to be at Ruth's keeping Nate company, making sure Ruth and her daughter were safe.

Slipping from beneath the sheets, Eric hiked up Sam's pajama bottoms and tried to figure out what he'd do for clothes. The bathroom clock read five something. And Eric wasn't the only one awake.

Rosa sat at a computer in the kitchen. She'd fixed her long hair in a braid and wore a fuzzy pink robe. She'd been his big sister's best friend and later his best friend. A black-and-white cat stretched out next to the computer monitor, unmindful of her typing.

She didn't turn but said, "Your clothes are folded on the chair over there."

He hurried back to the guest room and dressed in record time. Returning to the kitchen, he asked, "Is there any way to reach Nate?"

Rosa took a cell phone from next to her mouse pad, hit a key and handed him the phone. It took only a moment to ascertain that Ruth was fine and just as awake as they were. Nate even knew what all three ladies in the house were doing. Carolyn and Megan were sleeping, probably peacefully, and Ruth was surfing the Net, probably doing exactly what Rosa was doing—reading up on the Mallerys.

Eric had no more than hung up when Sam padded into the room. "It's not even six," he complained.

"It's your day off," Rosa said, "and you might as well face the truth. You're about to work your tail off."

Sam pulled a chair over to the computer. "So what have you found about the Mallerys?"

"The parents died in a cave-in."

Eric wanted to go closer, peer over her shoulder, see what she was seeing. "A cave-in? How did that happen?"

"They apparently were great hikers and liked to explore. They left the beaten path and didn't come home to make dinner for their sons one Saturday morning. Searchers found them a few hours later. They'd fallen into an old tunnel."

"Probably one of the Chinese ones we keep hearing about," Eric said.

"Probably," Rosa agreed. "Had they landed differently, they'd have lived and escaped. But they both broke their necks in the fall."

Against his will, Eric almost felt sorry for the Mallery brothers, including Benjamin. "What else did you find?"

"Did you know your sister, Mary, still owns the used-car lot?"

"No."

"Did you know Lucille Straus liked to steal cars?"

"No." This time both Eric and Sam answered, in unison.

Before Rosa could drop any more bombshells, the phone rang. Sam answered and gave three yeses and one okay before hanging up. "Mitch is busy in Wickenburg. He can't make breakfast and wants us to meet him for supper around six at the Last Chance Café."

Rosa turned from the computer. "Anything else?"

Sam looked at Eric. "Yeah, we're to make sure you and Ruth stay clear of Broken Bones. Mitch says if you so much as stray near city limits, he'll have you arrested."

"For what?" Eric sputtered. "I'm not under any restraining order."

"No, you're not," Sam agreed. "But they're doing something at the scrap yard and want to attract as little attention as possible. Someone seems to be keeping an eye on you and Ruth. Mitch wants you safe and out of the way for now. I know Mitch. He gets what he wants. He would have you arrested, and by the time your lawyer freed you, you'd have wasted precious hours in jail."

"I hate jail," Eric growled.

The phone rang again. This time Rosa snatched it, giving Sam a look that said, *Don't you dare!*

"It's Nate," she announced, then quickly returned to the call. "We're up. Yeah, Mitch just called. Sure, we'll come over for breakfast."

Sam was not a morning person. If Eric knew the way to Ruth's, he'd have jogged over. As it was, a good hour passed before they finally pulled in Ruth's driveway.

Carolyn proved to be a master chef. She made ham and cheese omelets, hash browns and freshly squeezed orange juice. "I hurried to the store before you got here," she confided to Eric.

Megan apparently had the only appetite of the bunch. She also had the only good mood. Rosa, at Sam's urging, drank two glasses of orange juice and stared longingly at Carolyn's coffee. Ruth picked at her meal and fidgeted, Megan chattered on about show-and-tell, recess, and about how some little boy named Manny kept bugging her.

Manny must not have bugged her too much, Eric thought a little while later, after Manny and his mother picked up Megan for school. The minute Megan closed the door, Rosa filled everyone in with what she'd discovered about the Mallery parents.

Ruth shook her head sadly. "Those poor boys. How old were they?"

To everyone's surprise, it was Carolyn who knew the answer. "Rich was twenty-one. He was in his third year of college. Benny was fifteen. He'd never been known for having both oars in the water. And after his parents' deaths, most people said neither oar ever touched the water again."

"How can you remember all this, Mom?"

"I remember how old I was when the Santellises moved their chop shop to the scrap yard. Benny had turned eighteen and knew the business. Rich was ecstatic that his brother wanted the family business. He returned to college and Benny turned to a life of crime. Oh, he'd dabbled in crime since grade school, but after finding his parents' bodies, he joined forces with the Santellises an—"

"Whoa," Eric said, "what do you mean finding his parents' bodies?"

"Benny knew where his parents liked to go on their hikes. He and Doc found their bodies. He was never the same after."

Nate had been quiet, now he spoke up, "Don't feel too sorry for him. Crime is a choice. He made the wrong one."

Glancing around the breakfast table, Ruth figured they were all guilty of wrong choices. Rosa said the words, Ruth couldn't yet form. "We're all sinners. No saints here."

Nate raised an eyebrow but his cell phone rang before he had time to respond. A moment later, he threw his napkin on the table and said, "Gotta scoot." Before he left, he looked at Ruth and Eric and gave strict orders. The same ones Mitch had. "You are not, I repeat, not to go near Broken Bones."

"He can be bossy," Rosa said, "but he really came through. He gave at least ten pages more than the original medical examiner did."

"Dustin's body…" She glanced at Ruth for permission to continue.

"I'm fine," Ruth said.

"…was probably moved right before Eric arrived. Nate said Dustin's skeleton was pretty much intact, and nothing was missing. That leads us to believe that until someone left his remains in Eric's shed, Dustin spent the last few years in a body bag."

"That would certainly make him easier to move," Eric said. "You think somebody drove up to the shed and dropped him off?"

"Yes," Sam spoke up, "and Nate thinks that Lucy surprised him. Whoever planned to leave Dustin's body, probably to lead suspicion to the Santellises, wound up killing Lucy because they didn't know she was living in the shed."

"If only the sheriff and twenty million vehicles hadn't messed up Eric's driveway. They checked every tire tread. Without exception they belonged to someone there after the fact."

"Does Nate think," Ruth said, "that Eric was the one being framed or that whoever did this was trying to cast suspicion on his brothers?"

"Can we rule out his brothers?" Carolyn cast a furtive look at Eric.

"Not entirely," Sam said, "but they're no longer the favorites."

"Why not?" Eric asked.

"Because of Lucy and the fact that the M.E. believes both Lucy and Dustin were killed with the same gun. There's not a chance that your brothers killed her. Sardi and Tony were dead. You were in prison. And, there's no indication that Kenny is in the area."

"So, who do they think killed Lucy now? And why, early on in the game, were they so willing to blame you, Rosa?" Carolyn started clearing up the breakfast dishes.

"I have to admit," Sam said, "there was plenty of evidence to support Rosa's guilt. Homeless people trust no one. She would have trusted Rosa enough to let her close. She'd made that shed her home. The clothes you were tossing aside, Eric, they were hers. There's bedding, papers, all kinds of things with her fingerprints on them."

"Her purse was most damaging," Rosa said. "My prints were not only on it, but also on the money inside."

"Then," Sam continued, "Sheriff Mallery started spouting off about the small bullet hole in her skull looking like the kind a Beretta 21 would make. Plus the bullet was missing and a nurse would know how to remove a bullet."

"Heads turned to look at me," Rosa said sadly. "I love that little Beretta, but it keeps getting me in trouble."

"Besides helping the authorities figure out that whoever is teamed up with Benjamin is still in the area," Sam said, "the bullet holes on your truck changed some minds about Rosa."

"Why?" Eric asked.

"Because," Sam said, "the bullet holes Dustin and Lucy sustained are not only small, but they're also somewhat oddly shaped."

"Same as the ones in your truck," Rosa added.

"Oddly shaped because they're homemade," Sam mused. "The coroners missed it at first, which is why one said same gun and the other said different gun. There was never any question about direction of fire. They only worried about the dimension of the hole."

Eric pushed aside what was left of his breakfast. "Who still makes homemade bullets? While we have plenty of skirt people around here, I don't see them as being so backward they'd make their own bullets."

"Skirt people?" Carolyn asked.

"People who survive on the outskirts of society. They don't fit in, don't want to, they're the ones who barricade themselves from society. They are usually some type of extremist."

Ruth knew where the skirt people lived. Broken-down

houses and broken-down people all calling Broken Bones home.

"I don't think they're responsible. I think we need to look at the sheriff. Almost every cop I work with is a gun addict. Rich Mallery is no different." Ruth started helping her mother. "What do you think?"

"Every gun enthusiast I know, and I know the same ones you do, can't wait to brag about what they do or have," Sam said. "Mitch has already exhausted that lead."

"Okay, I'll put Rich Mallery on a back burner, but believe me, I want to know more about him." Ruth looked at her watch. "So, what do we do next? I want to do something constructive."

"What's next," Eric said, "is we keep trying to find whoever is helping Benny. Ruth's right. We need to concentrate on the homemade bullets." He pulled the list out of his pocket and smoothed it on the table. It had gotten wet, horribly wrinkled, but was still legible.

Land
Lucy
Dustin
Mallerys
Ruth
Nate
Root Cellar
Mallery's Scrap Yard

Ruth peered over his shoulder. By the look on her face, he knew she was thinking his list vastly inadequate when compared to her now-sodden notebooks.

Rosa pulled the list into the middle of the table so they

could all see. "Land won't help us with the bullets," she mused. "Lucy's a possibility, though. I'd think Native Americans capable of making a homemade bullet. Sam?"

"Then why haven't I arrested a Native American using homemade bullets?"

Ruth agreed. "Dustin never talked about homemade bullets, either. What else do we have? We're putting the Mallerys on a back burner. Skip me, skip Nate, skip the root cellar. What about the scrap yard? Bullets are made from lead? Is a scrap yard a good place to get lead?"

"A good scrap yard would have access to any material," Eric said. "But we need to put that on a back burner, too, at least until they let us return to Broken Bones. Plus, Mitch and his men are there right now. Ruth, why don't you call him and just mention the homemade-bullet angle?"

"Okay, we've got some ideas. I like that," Ruth said. "Let's go ahead and start with Lucille. It's the first hit we had on your list." She turned to Sam and Rosa. "Why don't you head to the reservation, see if you can locate any of Lucille's family, friends, try to find out why she might have been homesteading in Eric's shed."

"I'm not sure I'm the right choice," Rosa protested. "For a while, I was the number-one suspect in her death."

"I think you're the perfect choice," Ruth said. "You personally knew Lucille, you're visibly pregnant, which will evoke sympathy, and you're trying to help. Plus, Sam speaks Navajo."

Next, Ruth turned to her mother. Carolyn had been quiet for the last thirty minutes, as if afraid making her presence known might interfere. "Mom, I want you to go home, get on the Internet, find out not only how to make homemade bullets, but also make a list for me of gun clubs that have members from Broken Bones and Gila City.

"Also," Ruth went on, "I know you still have a couple of friends in Broken Bones. Call them. See what they know about homemade bullets."

"Wait," Sam said. "I don't think that's a good idea. She could ask the wrong person."

"I know who to ask," Carolyn said. "And they won't think a thing of it. I'll be careful."

"Would you also pick up Megan at three?"

"Of course."

Last, Ruth turned to Eric. "We'll go to Phoenix. That's where they took the bodies. I know the coroner there, and he'll talk to me. There's got to be some tiny thread of evidence we're missing. And obviously they've discovered a few things since they passed on Dustin's autopsy results to me."

"You don't need to go that far," Rosa said.

Sam completed her thought. "Nate called in a friend of his, a pathologist. He's retired, he's in Wickenburg, and he was able to examine both Lucy and Dustin. He's the one who said same gun while the county coroner said different gun. Terry Anderson is technically a pathologist who specializes in postmortem chemistry."

Ruth wrote down the address, and like that, breakfast was over. Sam and Rosa took off in their car. Ruth's mom took off in her car, and that left Eric and Ruth standing in front of the tricolored Mustang.

"It's back to you and me," Ruth said softly.

"Seems to be working." The look in his eye indicated he was talking about more than crime investigation.

TWENTY-THREE

If Broken Bones was a wink on the highway of life then Gila City was a sneeze, and Wickenburg rated as a lazy wave. It boasted a population of over six thousand.

Terry Anderson, a retired pathologist who now made extra money giving expert testimony, lived off a dirt road but in a neighborhood that was quickly becoming residential. His wife opened the door and ushered Ruth and Eric into a living room that looked like a room out of a Zane Grey novel.

"Sam called and told us you were coming," Mrs. Anderson said. "Terry's out back."

She stared at Eric with an expression that appeared half terror, half awe.

"Thank you, ma'am."

Mrs. Anderson nodded. "I'll bring you both some iced tea."

Out back was another dirt road, some wild apple trees and lots of noise. Seems that during retirement, Terry Anderson had taken up a hobby. The lathe whirled while he expertly cut a groove in a piece of wood. He finally looked up, saw them and motioned for them to wait a minute.

"Makes sense," Ruth said. "Rocking chairs. He's a pathologist who likes to put things together."

Terry Anderson turned off the lathe and came over. He shook Ruth's hand but didn't take Eric's.

"I was wondering when you might show up," he said to Ruth. "I read the obit on your husband. He must have been a fine man. I'm sorry about your loss."

"We just want to make sure no one else gets killed."

Most people would have nodded at Ruth's statement, not Terry Anderson. Instead he sized up Eric while he continued to speak to Ruth. "Sure surprises me you're working with a Santellis."

"Not just any Santellis," Ruth said. "A Santellis who's never committed a crime, a Santellis who's worked on an undercover operation and helped put at least one drug lord out of business, and a Santellis who's served more than two years in prison for a crime he didn't commit."

When had being uncomfortable felt so comforting?

Eric cleared his throat and said, "I take it you know my family—"

"Everyone knows your family," Terry interrupted. He clearly didn't feel chastised by Ruth's comments.

"Intimately," Eric finished.

"I was county coroner for quite a few years before I retired. I cleaned up a few messes your family left behind. You'll pardon me if I don't welcome you."

"We learned some new information this morning." Ruth jumped into the conversation, probably thinking she was saving Eric. She wasn't. He would rather hear the truth from an honest man than accept a snub from a dishonest man. "You and the current coroner have determined both Lucy and my husband were killed by homemade bullets from the same gun. Since this wasn't in the autopsy report I was given, I want to know what else you've discovered."

About that time, his wife appeared with the tea glasses. Terry thanked her, sat down and took a drink.

Eric and Ruth followed his example.

"Two things bother me," Terry said, "but neither belong on an autopsy report. One, because there's no way we can prove it. It's strictly hearsay."

Ruth leaned forward.

"One of the deputies mentioned how your husband's body was laid out. At the time, no one really thought anything of it, but that's because we hadn't yet determined that Dustin was brought to the shed courtesy of a body bag."

"How my husband's body was laid out?" Ruth said slowly. "What do you mean?"

"Well, one would suppose the contents of a body bag would be somewhat dumped. Dustin's body wasn't dumped. Whoever put him in the shed was very careful when they took him out of the bag. They gently laid him out, and they knew what they were doing. It's as if they treated your husband with reverence."

"And you couldn't find a fingerprint, a fragment, something to give you a clue," Ruth said tersely.

"I don't know what *I* might have found had I been first at the scene. All I know is that by the time Nate arrived on the scene, it was contaminated beyond hope. If you had anyone but Nate helping you, the body bag would have been missed."

"What do you mean?"

"Nate's instincts are the best in the business. He determined by the rate of deterioration and completeness of the skeleton that Dustin spent a good deal of time in a body bag."

"Who in the area had access to body bags?"

"Rich Mallery, probably. Doc. Some think your friend Rosa. And, we're still not sure whoever moved the body was from the area."

"Why do you suppose they took Dustin out of the body bag," Ruth asked.

"Because maybe the body bag could be traced."

"What else bothers you?" Eric asked.

"Lucille Straus," Terry said easily. "She's full Navajo. Their customs demand immediate burial. Also, what was done to her body during the autopsy went against a dozen Native American taboos, yet no one raised a fuss. Besides the police, no one asked about her autopsy report. That girl didn't matter to anyone, not before she was murdered and not after. You never get used to something like that." He shook his head in disgust. "She wasn't even laid out in the shed as considerately as Dustin."

"But Dustin was dead when they arranged him. She was found in the exact position she died in."

"Another detail to prove I'm right. Whoever shot her, knew she was inside the shed dying, yet left her. Dustin died instantly. More humane. And here's the final kicker." Terry swirled the ice in his tea. "She's still not buried. The M.E. released her body, but no one has claimed it."

His tea glass empty and his mind full, Eric stood. He wanted to offer his hand but didn't.

"Where are you headed?" Terry asked, also standing.

"Where is her body?" Eric asked. He was somewhat surprised when Terry answered.

"Mitch had it moved to a funeral home over in Oxenburger."

"Why?" Ruth now stood, looking at Eric, and frowning.

"One, he was hoping by moving it closer, he'd make it easier for somebody to claim the body. Two, well, he'll never admit to it, but if another day or two goes by without someone claiming the body, Mitch will see she gets a proper burial, even if it's a white man's burial."

Eric's opinion of Mitch raised a notch or two. "Is there a chance we'd find out anything new if we went to the funeral home?"

"Doubtful," Terry said. "The funeral home is merely providing storage. It's also not like any funeral home you've ever seen. It's more or less a chapel, and all that's left of Lucille Damaris Straus now, thanks to the autopsy, is a snowy white skeleton, in a body bag instead of a casket, waiting for justice."

"How sad. How very sad." Ruth finally stood. "I never really considered what happened to Lucy. It never occurred to me that she'd have no one to mourn her."

"The lonely are easy to kill," Terry said.

Eric felt the first prickles of awareness. He'd been lonely, until he'd stumbled onto Lucy's body, until Ruth and Doc made his front porch their hangout, until Ruth dragged him into one more criminal investigation.

But Ruth wasn't done. "Thank you for the tea," she told Mr. Anderson. Then she surprised Eric by saying, "You know, Mr. Anderson, for three years I've blamed the Santellises for my husband's murder. I cannot even begin to describe the hatred I felt for them. But, today, I can't begin to describe how I feel about one of them." She looked at Eric. "One of them, I'd trust with my life."

"Then you must fear for your life," Terry said drily.

"No, I have a five-year-old daughter, and I'm a cop. I'm clutching at life with both hands and am just now learning how to live again."

Eric looked at her. He liked that she stood up for him. He liked her.

Once she settled in the passenger side, Ruth made two phone calls. The first one was to her mother. Carolyn shared all kinds of information about molds, muskets, rifles, pistols, the conical bullet and lead poisoning. She was just getting off the Internet and about to start calling her friends in Broken Bones. She sounded like a teenager getting ready to go on a first date.

Rosa answered her cell phone. They weren't even to the reservation yet, but Rosa agreed to make finding out why Lucy was unclaimed a top priority.

After hanging up, Ruth had Eric stop at a convenience store. She grabbed a soda and a new, very overpriced notebook. Eric filled up the tank and purchased a map of the area. Oxenburger wasn't even on it.

Ruth took out Eric's cell phone again—she'd never returned it—and called Terry Anderson, got directions, and in just a few minutes they were on their way.

Because of yesterday's rain it took longer than necessary to get to Oxenburger, a little burg off the beaten path. It claimed a population of 310. The town basically was a post office, a small market and a Realtor. Oh, and of course, Ruth noted, a bar. It was the only establishment with patrons inside.

The Oxenburger Funeral Home was a few miles past the post office. A huge sign advertising the Oxenburger

Ranch spelled out how and why Oxenburger still existed. The homes and town serviced the ranch employees.

Terry Anderson hadn't exaggerated. It was a funeral home like none Ruth had ever seen. Clearly, at one time it had been a family dwelling, a very small family dwelling. And, clearly, it didn't cater to deceased individuals who might encourage a crowded viewing. There were no cars in the driveway and no one answered Ruth and Eric's knock. The phone number on the door plaque took Ruth to a recording that said to direct any questions to the Oxenburger Ranch.

"I've never been on a real ranch," Ruth said. "Have you?"

"Not lately."

Unlike the town, the Oxenburger Ranch was a thriving community. A man on a tractor waved. A group of Hispanic men stacking hay ignored them. Two children played on a swing set, unmindful of the heat that had erased all evidence of yesterday's rain. Ruth didn't even bother to count the dogs. She wasn't here to serve a warrant or arrest anybody. Plus, with Eric by her side, she felt safe.

"Wish we had your truck," Ruth muttered after looking at all the farm trucks they parked next to.

"Ah, we're going to make a Ford girl out of you yet."

The children stopped playing and ran inside. A moment later, before Ruth and Eric had time to do anything besides walk to the sidewalk, a woman, wiping her hands on a dish towel, stepped outside. "How can I help you?" she asked. The two children peeked around her.

"We just came from the funeral home." Ruth stepped toward the door, noticing how the woman's face changed from inquisitive to sensitive. "We need to talk to whoever is in charge."

The woman scooted her children back toward the swing set and beckoned Ruth and Eric inside. "That would be me."

Ruth pulled out her badge. "I'm hoping for some information concerning Lucille Straus."

"Oh, my!" The woman's hand went to her mouth. The dish towel fell to the ground. "You're Ruth Atkins. I'm so pleased to meet you. Mitch talks about you all the time."

"Mitch Williams talks about me all the time?"

"Well, he did until a few months ago. I'm Trudy Oxenburger. My husband owns this ranch and the funeral home. At one time it was just a family plot. It grew as the ranch grew. Of course, it's mostly for family and workers and the few weekenders who choose to stay here even after they've passed on."

"Except for Lucy Straus," Eric said.

Trudy's smile slid somewhat. Ruth could see a sadness underneath the personality.

"No, there are a few other people buried on our land. We help Mitch out."

"Why? Is he related?" Ruth asked.

"No," Trudy admitted, "but I owe him.

"Let me show you." Trudy left the room. A moment later she returned holding a set of keys. "Why don't you follow me to the funeral home?" She gathered her kids and hustled them to a brand-new truck. A late-morning visit to the place of graves didn't seem to bother them in the least.

A few minutes later they arrived at the funeral home. The two kids took off for the back. "I keep waiting for them to tire of looking at the old tombstones," Trudy shared, "but they're still amazed that the first inscription is from 1861." Instead of unlocking the church, she followed the kids to the back. Ruth looked at Eric, shrugged and followed. There were maybe thirty graves, more than half resembling something out of an Old West movie complete with falling-down stones and cacti.

"Come look," the little boy shouted. He aimed his order at Eric. Even though she wasn't invited, Ruth tagged along. The boy, probably in third or fourth grade, stood at the corner of the cemetery lot. There were two rustic graves surrounded by weathered wooden fences. "No one knows who they are," the boy whispered.

"Mitch is fascinated by them," Trudy said. "I thought for a while he'd demand they be exhumed."

"Cops hate the not knowing," Ruth whispered.

The boy came over to her and whispered, "Mr. Mitch always whispers when we stand here, too."

"So," Ruth said, maybe a bit too loudly, "How did you and Mitch become friends?"

"*Friends,*" Trudy said, "is not quite the word." She led them to the middle of the plot. There were three graves there, all new, all with flat markers.

"Cases Mitch worked on," Trudy said. "Unclaimed bodies."

"Why let them be buried here?"

Trudy moved to the left, a single grave, surrounded by highly decorated wrought iron fencing. Ruth leaned forward and read: Janice Tate, 1975–2004, *…was lost and is now found. So they began to celebrate. Luke 15:24*

"My sister," Trudy explained. "One of the 220 people murdered in the Phoenix area that year. Mitch found out who killed her well after others stopped searching. I'll be forever grateful."

Ruth was silent, thinking about loss, thinking about God, thinking about Luke 15:24. She'd always equated her search for Dustin's killer to the widow with the lost coin, but maybe the lost son was better. After all, Dustin was only dead to the earth, not to the Father.

He'd gone home.

Ruth would see him again.

Over lunch, which Trudy insisted on, she filled them in on her sister's murder and on the other three people Mitch had helped bury in Oxenburger, and on Lucille Straus.

What Eric couldn't forget were Terry Anderson's words about the lonely being easy to kill and, judging by how much time Lucy had spent here at the Oxenburger Funeral Home, they were also easy to forget.

"Isn't there a time restriction," he asked, "about how soon a body must be interred?"

"If not for the ongoing investigation, we'd have buried her two days after you buried Dustin," Trudy said. "And, you're right. I'm uncomfortable. Poor girl. She's like Janice, and we're waiting for justice."

Ruth's cell phone, make that Eric's, rang. Eric watched as she answered, checked her watch, started getting agitated, and said, "No, I'm glad you called. What time again?" Ruth took her notebook from her purse. Opened it and managed to balance a cell phone on her shoulder while writing notes. When she hung up, she also stood up. She hurriedly plugged a number into her phone, waited a moment, tapping her foot the whole time, and then hung up before announcing, "We need to go."

"Who was that?" Eric asked.

"You remember my mom's friend in Broken Bones. Well, no, of course you don't. Pixie Butler. Mom was supposed to meet her for lunch."

"When?"

"An hour ago, at The Last Chance Café."

"Your mom likes to disappear," Eric reminded Ruth. "Are you sure we need to worry?"

"She wouldn't disappear now," Ruth said firmly.

"And you should always worry when someone disappears," Trudy Oxenburger whispered.

TWENTY-FOUR

They were in Eric's borrowed car and heading for Broken Bones, Mitch's orders ignored, in a matter of seconds. Trudy Oxenburger's words followed Eric out the door and into the car.

People disappeared all the time.

Like his sister.

And you should always worry when someone disappears.

As soon as they figured out who Dustin's killer was, Eric was going to devote his time to finding Mary. He knew how now. Thanks to Ruth. He listened as she started a series of phone calls. The first was to Mitch. No one answered. "He has to be somewhere out of service," she said, and wrote in her notebook. A moment later, she added, "Nate's not picking up, either." Next, she tried Rosa, who did answer. Quickly Ruth filled her in on Pixie's phone call, and Eric finally got to hear the rest of the details.

Clutching the phone in a death grip, the words spilled out of Ruth's mouth. "I guess Mom called Pixie right before noon. Pixie couldn't think of anyone who made homemade bullets but told Mom that she should talk to either Axel or John Billings, who owns the Last Chance Café. Pixie remembered that they had bullet molds on their walls. Mom thought it was a great idea and took it a step further. She invited Pixie to meet her for lunch at the Café. Only, Mom never showed."

Eric couldn't hear Rosa's reply but he knew Rosa and Sam well enough to know they'd be sprinting to their car as soon as the call ended.

Ruth sniffed and ever the professional asked, "Did you find out anything about Lucy?"

She turned the page of her notebook and wrote whatever it was Rosa was saying. When she finally hung up, Eric started to say, "Wha—" but Ruth was already dialing a new number. One thing for sure, Eric knew, cops had as many tricks up their sleeve as criminals. Ruth got hold of her captain at the Gila City Police Department and asked him to find out what calls had been made from her house this morning.

After hanging up, she carefully placed the phone on the console between them and said, "Lucille's family is gone. She had no siblings and no friends. When I got hold of Rosa, Sam was filling out some forms at the Indian Affairs office. Seems that with all the hoopla, the news of Lucy's demise might have slipped through the cracks. Rosa also said it would take them a while to get to Broken Bones and to wait for them. She also said to call Mitch."

"What do you want to do?" He already knew the answer.

"Head for Broken Bones. Let's see what we can find out."

She tried both Mitch and Nate two more times. She called Pixie again, but Pixie still hadn't heard from Carolyn.

Two weeks away from the force, and already Ruth was stretching the boundaries of what she knew was right. She'd allowed her mother to help because her mother was the best choice. Wrong. Ruth knew better. She tried her mom's cell phone again. Nothing. Just when she thought she was willing to get out of the Mustang and push if it would get them to Broken Bones faster, the phone rang. Good thing a warrant wasn't necessary for someone who wanted their own phone records. The captain provided three names and numbers. None were a surprise.

"Here's the order." Ruth wrote them in her notebook even as she said them aloud. "Pixie was first. That call was about 11:00 a.m., just like Pixie said. Then, Mom called the Axel Pruitt residence. That was at 11:09 a.m. She didn't let any time waste, that's for sure."

"Why did she call the residence instead of the bar?" Eric asked.

"She used to clean the bar, early in the morning. I'd tag along. Axel's wife would bring us breakfast. She'd get more info from the wife than the husband. He'd want a twenty just for saying hello."

"Number three."

"No surprise, she called the Winterses. Elizabeth knows more about guns than most people. That was at 11:15 a.m."

Quickly dialing the phone, Ruth waited impatiently for Tamela Pruitt to answer. If Axel was a hundred, then Tamela had ten years on him. Finally the gravelly voice came on the phone. "I told your mother," Tamela drawled, "that the bullet molds on our walls came from Doc and Elizabeth Winters. When Doc had his trouble, Elizabeth offered to sell us some of her antiques. We were thrilled to get them."

Ruth hung up, repeated the conversation to Eric, and settled back in her seat. Boy, she needed her notebook. She'd written a few things about the Winterses inside the one titled Broken Bones and now something tickled her memory. What was it? She quickly dialed the Winterses.

Great, no answer.

"Why do you suppose your mother didn't call the Last Chance Café?" Eric asked.

"Because she was meeting Pixie there. Why call if you're going to go?"

"Tell me what you're thinking?" Eric asked.

"Something about the Winterses. Something Ricky said that time we were all at the café. Doc got sued five years ago. That was about the time he retired. If he lost a lawsuit and then retired…"

"How do you explain the upgrade to the cabin?" Eric finished for her. "And all the money it would take?"

"He'd still have money," Ruth muttered. Suddenly bits and pieces of conversation came to mind. The number of stolen cars doubling during the last five years. Terry Anderson talking about the fingerprints they'd lifted, Doc's being predominant; Doc's announcement in the shed about a Beretta 21. It was as if *he'd purposely aimed suspicion at Rosa.*

Why? What had Rosa done to him?

Then, there was Doc's continued presence. Was it curiosity and time on his hands as he claimed? Or had he been there because he knew something and wanted to make sure nobody else became privy to the information. It made sense. Doc had been included on every step.

The Winterses lived close to the scrap yard.

"They're involved." She turned to Eric. "They're probably doing what my mother did. Doc knows everybody. Everybody trusts him."

Maybe the Winterses needed money, the kind of money a chop shop could provide. Money could convince a man, even a doctor to become a snitch, but who was he snitching to?

She closed her eyes, opened them, stared at Eric. "You know, I can even remember him asking one of those curiosity-seekers, who drove by your cabin right after you found Dustin, what year his BMW was."

It paid to be a cop. She stayed on the cell phone all the way to Broken Bones. She found out the renovations to the cabin had started just four years ago. She found out about the Winterses fixing up their home and about Elizabeth's medical bills. She found out exactly how much they'd lost in the lawsuit and exactly how much they'd had left. She found out enough to make her stomach hurt.

If it looks like a duck and quacks like a duck...

They also weren't answering their phone. Just as Ruth was about to try Mitch's cell phone again, the distant sound of thunder rolled. "Perfect," Eric muttered.

Ruth dialed Rosa, who appeared to be the only person on the face of the earth, besides the captain at the Gila City Police Department, answering the phone today. "Don't go there," Rosa ordered, after Ruth spilled everything she'd found out. "Let me call the police."

"Do it," Ruth urged. "Tell them everything I've told you. Tell them to find Mitch Williams and get him to the Winterses' place."

"Don't go there," Rosa repeated.

"It's my mother."

"Rosa's right," Eric said after Ruth hung up. "We don't

have to go there. You have a daughter. One who needs to be picked up from school in a few hours. If the Winterses are involved, and I agree with you, I think they are, we don't know the situation we'll be walking into. We need to tread carefully."

"Tread carefully!" she shrieked. It felt good. "I've trod carefully. For three years! And now you want me to wait until we can get hold of Mitch, until we can get hold of one of the deputies who helped destroyed the crime scene, until we can get hold of someone who doesn't know Dustin or care about Lucy, until—"

"This is no longer just about Dustin or Lucy," Eric said softly. "Right now it's about your mother and finding out where she is."

"We're going to the Winterses'," Ruth said. "I'm not losing my mother, too!"

The second thunder boom was so loud, Ruth jumped. Rain hit the window, a few blobs at a time, quickly merging into a downpour. Prospector's Way was the next turn. Even with the wipers going—they actually worked— Ruth could barely make out the road. It wasn't paved. It didn't look welcoming.

Pulling into the front yard of his cabin, Eric was struck by the isolation of it all. The cabin had been so lonely when he first arrived, all his belongings stashed in a used truck. Then, it had been a hotbed of activity. Now, it was back to being lonely again. He almost felt sorry for the cabin. Until Ruth entered his life, he'd felt sorry for himself.

"Why are we stopping?" Ruth asked.

"My gun."

She looked at him. He could see the first inkling of anticipation cross her face. This wasn't a game and she wasn't an observer. "I don't have mine," she said softly. "All these years of carrying it as easily as I carry a purse, and I don't have it today."

"You never carried it easily," he said. "You do a better job with the notebooks than the gun. In your case, the pen *is* mightier than the sword."

She didn't answer, which told him he was right.

"Still time to change your mind," he said. "You know the importance of backup, and I'm all you got. That's not much."

"It's enough."

He'd known her two weeks. He'd had library books in his possession longer than that and hadn't minded returning them. She was different. He said the words, even though he'd promised himself he wouldn't, yet. "You know, if I weren't a Santellis—"

"If you weren't a Santellis, you wouldn't have to ask."

It said everything. It changed nothing.

His gun was tucked away in the fireplace. It felt cold and hard, like his old life: a life that wasn't that long ago or far away. He stuffed the gun in the back of his pants and hurried outside. Ruth waited, looking anxiously at the road and the rain, back at the road and then finally at him. "I still can't get hold of Mitch," she said nervously as he took his place behind the wheel.

The moment Eric turned the Mustang onto Prospector's Way and toward the Winterses' place, he started thinking of all the reasons why they should *not* be doing this. There were a million. None convincing enough to sway Ruth.

Okay, they were going to the Winterses' place. He didn't like it, but he accepted it, and he even understood it. Parents did that to a person, made them take risks. Luckily, since he had control of the vehicle, he'd be on hand to make sure Ruth didn't take any chances. And, if Ruth even acted as though she wanted to get out of the car, he'd lock her in the trunk. He wouldn't let her take another foolish risk as she had yesterday.

His heart couldn't take it.

TWENTY-FIVE

This time, Ruth thought, the Winterses' cabin didn't look as inviting, as awe-inspiring, as it had just a few days earlier when they'd gone there for lunch.

The borrowed Mustang, just like Eric's truck, had a broken heater. Arizona wasn't supposed to be cold, ever. She shivered and stole another look at Eric. He'd pulled to the side of the road just before the Winterses' driveway and there they sat. The car was running, and his foot hovered near the gas pedal. He really didn't trust her. He'd said that if she tried getting out of the car, they'd be out of there. She frowned, hating that he was right, grateful that she was smart enough to listen.

Glancing at her watch, Ruth knew that at any minute the school bell would ring and Megan would join a line of children heading for the gym and after-school care.

Two hours wasn't enough, and Eric's cell phone was about out of juice. Ruth wondered if the phone inside the Winterses' cabin worked. Glancing, again, at the wooden structure, she tried to discern a light, movement, something. The Hummer was parked in the driveway. Doc's Cadillac was in front of it. Her mother's car wasn't in sight. Maybe it was parked in back, but Eric wasn't open to exploration-type suggestions.

"Look—" she began.

"The cops should be here any minute."

"I am a cop," she reminded him, not for the first time, "and I know enough to be careful. I just want to check the back, see if her car—"

"And you don't know what you'll find. You might make things worse."

She couldn't remember the last time… No, she could. The last time she'd felt this antsy, really, had been the night Dustin failed to come home, and she'd been stuck waiting for a phone call. She'd hated the feeling. It was part of the reason she'd become a cop. She didn't want to be the one waiting ever again; she wanted to be the one doing.

Where were the police? Why were they taking so long?

Picking up her notebook, she started sketching the cabin—more for something to do than the expectation of sudden insight. At first, her fingers flew across the page, then they slowed as she started savoring the similarities and differences between the Winterses', the Mallerys' and the Santellises' cabins. What a history the three families shared.

A few minutes later, she paused, something bothering her. "Hey." She sat up so fast the notebook fell to the floorboard. Snatching it up, she held it out so he could study it. "What do you see?"

"Oh, you're talking to me again, playing nice." He squinted at the drawing. "I see a shoe with fish for windows."

"What?" She snatched the notebook back and looked

at it herself. "This is not the time to joke! My mother's missing, really missing. Look here." She thrust the notebook at him again and pointed. "It's the shed. Like yours! All three of the cabins have one. Pretty much in the same place."

"So?"

"Well, it's freshly painted, and there's no gaping holes like yours has, but it's still old. It doesn't fit."

He looked past the parked cars, the scrubby trees, at the shed. "It is old. So what? Mine's old."

"That's not what I'm getting at. Why didn't they renovate the shed when they redid the cabin?"

"Maybe they didn't care?"

"Look at the cabin. They care."

Eric finally took his foot away from the gas pedal, turned off the ignition and paid attention. "Look, what's in your shed?"

"Not much, now."

"I'm talking about the root cellar. I'll bet they have one, too. That's why it still looks old. They couldn't hire a contractor without giving up their secrets."

Eric didn't comment, which only proved to Ruth how credible she sounded. She kept talking, thinking things through, out loud, the way she used to with Sam, her old partner, before he married Rosa. It felt good. "Let's go look, just at the shed. We gotta—"

"We *gotta* wait."

If not for the car pulling up behind them, she'd have argued. Eric was already opening the door and heading back to meet Rosa and Sam. Ruth followed on his heels. He got to them first because she slowed, slowed because she saw the look in Sam Packard's eyes.

"What is it?" She felt out of breath, and not from the rain or the rush of the day. "Are we going in? Are more people coming? Have they heard anything about my mother?"

Sam opened his mouth, about to speak, but a dull pop, loud enough to catch their attention, distant enough to make four people look four different ways, sounded.

"What was that?" Ruth turned, took a step and halted when Eric's hand closed on her elbow.

"You don't move toward gunshots," he warned. "You duck."

She wasn't in the mood to listen to him. Of that, Eric was sure. "That was a gunshot!" Ruth wiped rain off her brow.

"Yup," Rosa agreed.

Ruth lurched again, and Eric felt his hold give a little as she cried, "My mother might be in there!"

"In where?" Eric argued, wishing he'd put her in the trunk when he had a chance. "If that shot came from the shed, we'd have heard it clearly."

"I can't just wait here!"

Sam pulled out his gun, checked the chamber before reholstering it, and said, "Okay, let's do something."

The words were just what she needed, and Eric wished he'd said them. Ruth seemed to regroup there in front of him. Gone was the woman, the peer, he'd worked beside all day. She was replaced by Officer Ruth Atkins, badge number 743. She went to Sam, and Eric almost hated the man.

Rain pelted her, and she looked at Sam with the type of trusting expression Eric longed to see from her.

"Eric," Sam said after a moment, "you got a permit for the gun you're carrying?"

"Yes."

"Good enough for me. Ruth, you've been here before. Make the call."

She didn't even blink. "Rosa, you head back to town. Don't give up until you get hold of Mitch, Nate, anybody. Even those silly deputies. Also, call Megan's school, tell the principal what's going on. Ask him to see if the teacher or one of Megan's friends can watch her." She turned back to the men. "Sam, you check the doors and windows of the cabin. Eric, we're checking out the shed."

Sam stopped, a foot already on the front porch step. "Why do we need two people to check out a shed?"

Eric explained quickly, as Ruth gave some last-minute orders to Rosa.

Sam ran up the stairs and knocked on the cabin door. No one answered. Then, he tried peering in the windows before checking the perimeter of the cabin. Finally, he headed for the shed, catching up to Ruth and Eric.

The shed was open. It was smaller and cleaner than Eric's. Gardening tools lined one side. Crates, carefully labeled with words like *Xmas, Books,* etc were scattered about. The root-cellar opening was easy to find. The Winterses' obviously used theirs. Eric found the ring and pulled upward. A dull light spiraled out.

"Electricity," Sam said, surprised. "I'm going down first." He shot Ruth a look that dared her to argue. "Count to ten, then follow. I want to make as little noise as possible."

One, two…ten didn't seem as if it should be such a distance, but it was. Eric's foot was on the top step at eight.

Ruth's at nine. He reached the bottom of the stairs at ten. Ruth bumped into him. Sam stood in the middle of the empty room.

"But the light is on," Eric said softly.

"There is that," Sam agreed.

"I wanted her to be here," Ruth muttered. "I hate this not knowing."

Eric looked around. "The sound came from this way. We're missing something."

Step by step, Eric and Ruth went around the room telling Sam the similarities between the two sheds. It didn't take long. The Winterses' shed was half the size. The biggest difference was that the root cellar looked as if maybe it had actually once been used as a root cellar. Empty shelves, with plenty of cobwebs, lined almost all the walls.

"Anything else?" Sam asked.

"My shed had lots of Chinese clothes and stuff. Ruth and I thought that was unusual."

"And," Ruth added, "there were no shelves on this wall. There were claw marks. Like someone had dug their fingernails in."

"I agree, very unusual." Sam turned, studying each wall. "Nothing here. Let's—"

The ground quivered, just for a moment, and then came a series of loud thuds, followed by a long scream: a scream that came from the other side of the root cellar's walls. Not up aboveground.

"What the…" Sam said.

"That was my mother," Ruth said.

"You sure it wasn't Elizabeth Winters?" Eric asked.

Up above, a door creaked as someone entered the

shed. The sound of something dragging silenced the room. Eric looked at the entrance and pulled his gun. Elizabeth Winters's face appeared. "No, not Elizabeth Winters." He answered his own question.

"I can't do the stairs anymore," she said frantically.

"Stay up there," Sam advised.

Eric moved toward the stairs. "Elizabeth, did you recognize the noise? Where it came from?"

"The tunnels are collapsing somewhere, prob... probably because of the rain and the gun...gunshot." Tears, combined with a severe shortness of breath, made the words almost unintelligible. Elizabeth grasped the handrail and collapsed on the front step. "Doc's in there."

"Where's my mother, Mrs. Winters?"

Elizabeth looked at Ruth. Her mouth opened, no sound came out.

"How do we get in there?" Eric asked. When she didn't answer, he reminded her, "Doc's in there."

Elizabeth pointed, at the far wall. They all turned to look. It was dirt, packed hard and stained with age. "Go dead center," Elizabeth ordered, "grab the middle shelf, and pull."

Dead center, Eric thought. What an unfortunate choice of words. He and Sam both headed for the wall, aimed dead center and pulled. A door opened.

"Elizabeth, what is this?" Eric called.

"One eye of the Chinese tunnels. They run up and down Prospector Way."

"And your husband is in there because..."

She didn't answer. Just looked at Ruth sorrowfully.

"Yet you want us to go in there and save him?" Ruth asked.

"He's seventy-three years old! He might be hurt!"

"And does my mother also need rescuing?" Ruth demanded.

Weeping and avoiding Ruth's eyes, Elizabeth croaked, "Probably not."

Eric turned toward the tunnel. Darkness, the kind he'd never seen, bade do-not-enter. "We're going to need flashlights."

"I've got some out in the car," Sam said.

"I have two in my car," Ruth muttered. Lot of good they'll do. Her face was as pale as Eric had ever seen it.

Elizabeth managed to say, "Right when you enter you'll find lanterns on the left and flashlights on the right."

Sam went in first while Eric stared up at Elizabeth. He'd sat at her table thinking her honorable. She'd fooled him. He turned to Ruth. "Is there any chance at all I can convince you to stay here and watch her?"

"None."

"I was afraid of that." He turned back to Elizabeth. "Will you be all right while we go look for your husband?"

She nodded.

"Coming?" Sam called.

"Coming," Ruth answered.

Eric felt his teeth clench. He didn't like leaving Elizabeth. But he liked the idea of having Ruth out of his sight even less. Full darkness closed in after just a few steps. The flashlights were pinpoints into nothing. The rain was soundless inside the gloom of the tunnels, yet the dampness reminded Eric of where they were, where they were going. In just a little while he might very well be carrying out the body of Ruth's mother. And maybe Doc, as well.

Please, he prayed, *don't let anything happen to Ruth. Take me instead.* There, he'd done it. Said a prayer. And, yes, he did feel better. He only hoped it lasted.

A murky, dusty smell filled his nostrils. He'd never been a spelunker. And now, he never planned to. He liked having a right, left, forward, backward, escape plan, and he loved electricity. Down here there was only what was behind and what was ahead. He could really see neither. Every once in a while he thought he caught a sound, up ahead, but then the silence reasserted itself.

Next to him, Ruth tripped, put a hand out and said, "I can't even find a wall to help guide us."

Eric took her hand and held on. They turned a corner and suddenly didn't need their flashlights.

Carolyn George sat on the ground, a lantern next to her. In her lap, an unmoving Doc Winters. A few feet away stood Benjamin Mallery, holding a lantern in one hand a gun in the other. Benjamin's eyes never left Doc. "I didn't mean to kill him."

Ruth let go of Eric's hand and hung back, staring at her mother. Carolyn looked perfectly sane as she said to Eric. "He did it to save me," she said simply.

"Benjamin," Sam said, "What are you doing down here?"

"Trying to keep all you fool people away from me. You don't learn. I coulda hit more than your truck yesterday, but I knew Carolyn's daughter was in it. Fool people. Cops been searching my place for a week. 'Course, they ain't finding much. Seems the tunnels are the only safe place." He looked at Doc. "Only, they weren't so safe."

"Tamela told me about the gun molds," Carolyn said. "I thought Elizabeth could give me some more information. I never dreamed, I didn't think…."

"You use homemade bullets?" Sam asked, unable to keep the surprise out of his voice.

"Sure do. Mrs. Winters gave me a bunch. Showed me how to make them, too."

"It was Elizabeth all the time," Carolyn said softly.

"It's okay, Mom," Ruth said. "The Winterses fooled all of us."

"Doc brought me down here, pushed me, he had a gun. This is where they kept Dustin. He told me that and he told me he was going to shoot me."

"I couldn't let that happen," Benjamin said solemnly. "Carolyn's always been my friend."

Eric moved toward Carolyn while Sam moved toward Benjamin. Ruth knew both were thinking there were too many guns in the tunnel—an already shaky tunnel.

"You know what Doc said before he died?" Carolyn asked after Eric kicked Doc's gun away.

"Why don't you tell us," Eric urged.

Carolyn stroked Doc's hair. He'd been going to shoot her, but still, she stroked his hair. "He asked me to look after Elizabeth."

Beside him, he heard Ruth take a deep breath, and then came a sound he recognized. It was the sound of a woman trying not to lose it.

Sam looked at Benjamin. "Did Doc have any last words for you?" he asked.

Benjamin nodded. "Yeah, he said 'Don't shoot.'"

That's when Ruth lost it. "Mom," she said, sounding choked up. She didn't move, but held out her hand as if trying to break through an invisible wall. She took a step, and Eric held his breath.

Family, they made you crazy, and no matter what they did, they were yours.

"Mom," Ruth said again.

That's when the tunnel tilted, the ceiling fell and the darkness came.

TWENTY-SIX

The noise was deafening. A two-dollar flashlight suddenly became Eric's most valuable possession. Its beam was as shaky as he was. Huge chunks of dirt pounded at his feet, sending him scrambling backward and pulling Ruth's mother along with him. She was deadweight.

Another bad choice of words.

Carolyn finally let go of Doc and moved with Eric, half crawling, half running. Then came an eerie silence. Before a cave-in, Eric thought, there should be a trickle of warning: some small dirt clods falling down, the quivering of the ground like the time when they'd been in the root cellar. Something. Nope, not this time, not this cave-in. One moment Eric had been looking at Carolyn and Doc; the next moment, Eric stood in the darkness trying to get a head count: one, two, three. "Somebody's missing," he said.

"Ruth!" Carolyn called.

Sam added his voice, "Ruth!"

"She's not by me." Benjamin moved his flashlight around the area.

Eric hit the dirt where just moments before Ruth had

stood. He didn't find a shoe, a hand, anything. He clawed at the dirt, trying to move it, getting nowhere. After a moment, he realized that both Sam and Carolyn were doing the same.

"Ruth!" he screamed.

"That cave-in's a biggun," Benjamin said. "I'd say at least a solid week of digging."

"You don't think she's…" Carolyn George started weeping.

"Ruth!" Eric screamed her name as loud as he could. Nothing but the beleaguered silence responded. "Ruth! Ruth! Ruth!"

"This isn't helping," Sam said. "We need to get to her." He turned to Benjamin. "What do we do?"

"I kin take you to the closest eye. It's about a half-hour walk."

"Let's go," Eric said. "I'm thinking it's a twenty-minute run."

"I'm thinking there's a chance of other cave-ins," Benjamin responded.

Eric took out his gun and held it to his side. He hated the feel of its slickness, hated that his heart allowed him to handle a gun so easily. Benjamin didn't seem to care. He moved toward Carolyn and when Eric almost protested, she shook her head.

"You okay," Benjamin asked.

"Yes, thanks to you."

"I'll get us out of here," Benjamin promised.

"Good," Eric said. "Let's do it now." In the velvety blackness, he walked close to Benjamin. The man's flashlight bobbed a beam of light on the floor, the walls, the ceiling. Eric encouraged a half walk, half run.

Carolyn tripped once, fell on her hands and knees, and Sam helped her to her feet. She didn't complain, just kept on moving, meeting Eric's frantic pace in a darkness that made hurrying almost impossible.

As they followed Benjamin's flashlight, he began a monologue, seeming to need no response. Since the constant barrage of words seemed to calm Carolyn somewhat, Eric allowed it, but what he really wanted to do was yell, "Shut up! Ruth is hurt! Get us out of here. Now!"

Benjamin quickly pointed out old stuff, left over from miners and from the Chinese; he showed them the newer items, air bags that made him the most money and parts for both Mercedes and BMW vehicles.

"How long you been using the tunnels?" Sam asked.

"Just five years. It was Doc's idea really." Benjamin admitted. "He remembered them from when we found my parents. They were hiking our land and fell in a tunnel. But I didn't think much about them again until Doc suggested we work together."

"Elizabeth researched the tunnels for her book," Eric said. "So she knew what they were and how far-reaching they were."

Benjamin nodded. "She was too sick to explore much, though."

Slowly, Eric put away the gun. He couldn't hold it while praying to the Father about Ruth's safety. It felt wrong somehow. She had to make it out alive. She had a daughter and a mother who needed her. He needed her.

Benjamin had told the truth. It took thirty minutes to lead them to the closest eye of the tunnel, which turned out to be the root cellar in his shed.

"Does the tunnel lead to my shed, too?" Eric asked,

looking around a root cellar the exact same layout as the Winterses'. Only, this one was full of trash.

"To your old shed, the one that burned down. If you look where the old shed was, before it burned down, you can find the door," Benjamin said. "It's more or less part of the ground. I only been there once. Doc said it wasn't safe to hide anything here. Still too many Santellises running free. That's why I tried to buy your property before you moved in. Sure wish you'd have sold." He shot Eric a sad look. "Then, I'd own just about everything hereabouts and none of this would have happened."

"What?" Sam's words were spoken so sharply, Eric almost expected to hear more rumbling in the cave.

Benjamin stopped, confused. He was halfway up the stairs, and Eric bumped into him. "Until you showed up, I never had to kill nobody. Sure, we ran a chop shop, but nobody got hurt."

"Dustin Atkins was not a nobody," Sam said tersely.

"And neither was Lucille Straus," Eric added.

"You'll have to talk to Mrs. Doc about that," Benjamin said, exiting the shed and looking at the truck parked in front of his cabin. "Until the police started sniffing around the scrap yard, I had no clue they'd done the deeds." He looked at Eric, no fear in his eyes, and shook his head. "I blamed you and your brothers. Only person I ever killed was Doc."

Eric very much wanted to talk to Mrs. Doc. But first he wanted to talk to Ruth Atkins, and Benjamin's ramblings were slowing things down. "Where's your car?" Eric asked.

"Out front."

Two minutes later, they were on their way. Benjamin

had turned over his truck keys to Eric without protest. The road was muddy, but not enough to keep Eric married to the speed limit.

"You might want to slow down," Sam advised.

Eric opened his mouth to protest, but the sight of flashing lights silenced him. During the time they'd been leaving the cave the cavalry had arrived. There was a half dozen at least. One officer raised his hand for them to stop. Eric started to comply, but that's when he saw her. He was out of the truck and running before the officer had time to issue any orders.

He skidded to a stop just out of arm's reach. She wanted to rush toward him, unmindful of the mud covering him—it covered her, too—but she suddenly felt shy.

"I was worried," he said.

"Me, too."

"You're not hurt?" he asked.

"No, not even a scratch. I made it back to the root cellar in about five minutes."

Somebody brought Eric a blanket. Ricky the reporter walked their way, took one look and headed for Carolyn.

"I was so worried," Eric repeated.

"It's okay. I was terrified at first, until I found my way back to the root cellar. Then, I was mad because I wasn't with you guys. But, when I finally crawled out of the shed, I realized why God had sent me back."

"Why?"

"Mrs. Winters was still sitting on the top step. I thought for a moment she was dead."

"She wasn't?"

"No, and she was still asking if we'd found Doc."

"What did you tell her?"

"That the tunnel had collapsed, and everyone was on the other side, including Doc. Luckily, she didn't ask for details."

"We couldn't get him out. He's buried under a ton of mud."

"I think, even though I didn't tell her he was dead, she knew. She kept saying 'It's all over now.'"

"Did she say anything else?"

"She said that when you got out of jail and had the electricity at your place turned on, she and Doc decided to move Dustin's body. She said none of this was Doc's fault, and it bothered him that Dustin didn't get a proper burial and that I couldn't get past my grieving," Ruth said sadly. "They thought your brothers would be blamed and no one would even make much of a stink."

"Did she mention Lucy?" Eric asked.

"Lucy surprised Doc in the shed. He didn't realize she'd been squatting there. He hit her with a shovel, and then he came home and got Elizabeth. She said it didn't bother her to shoot Lucy. Once she had Doc retrieve the bullet, she just figured you'd get blamed. She said that five generations of her family had owned this land, and that next it was going to her oldest son. I guess they almost lost everything after Doc was sued, and she got so sick. Joining forces with Benjamin Mallery took them out of the red and into more money than Doc ever made with his small-town practice. I told her to stop talking, save her strength, but just as I got her to her bedroom she told me she'd shot Dustin."

And Eric took her in his arms, folding her in as if she

were a child, and holding her so close she could feel his heart beating through both his shirt and the blanket.

Tears misted Ruth's eyes. She rested her head on his shoulder and continued, "She said that at first, she didn't even know it was him. She just knew a cop had pulled over Doc, and Doc was in a stolen car. You know, she acted as if it were partly Dustin's fault, said he wasn't supposed to be in Broken Bones nosing around."

"What happened next?" Eric asked.

"I don't know," Ruth said. "I told her I didn't need to know the details. And for the first time in three years, I meant it. I had other things to worry about."

"Your mother and Megan," Eric agreed.

"And you."

Before she could say anything else, Mitch Williams tapped her on the shoulder. "Okay, you guys! I realize the happy reunion is needed, but there are plenty of questions to answer. You can get all cozy later."

"If I wasn't a Santellis…" Eric whispered.

"If you weren't a Santellis," Ruth whispered back, "you wouldn't be you."

She let go then, smiled at him and walked toward her mother. As he watched them embrace, he realized that finally, he was watching the other half of his heart.

Ruth hung up the phone and looked across the room at her mother.

Carolyn George finally noticed and came over. "What did the hospital say?"

"Mrs. Winters has pneumonia. She'll be there for quite a while, if she lives. I made sure the hospital got their children's numbers."

"Good." Carolyn nodded.

Looking around, Ruth noted that for the most part, the people gathered tonight were the same ones who'd gathered just two weeks ago. And, in some ways, for Ruth, this gathering did more to lay Dustin to rest than anything else she'd done.

Once the news broke, the casseroles starting arriving again. It was nine at night, but the Atkinses' house was lit up like the Fourth of July.

"On a school night, too," Megan kept chortling. She bit into a cookie and confided in Eric. "Did you know that both my mom and my grandmother were on the news? All three stations. And they kept hugging each other. I've never seen them hug each other so much."

"Better not let your mother know how much TV you watched tonight," Eric warned.

"Good idea." Megan dropped her cookie and ran off to tell Aunt Rosa about watching all three news stations but not to tell.

Ruth took Megan's place and turned off the TV. "Megan watches it too much," she confided.

"You might be right," Eric agreed.

There were fifty people in the house, but for Ruth, sitting next to Eric, there was really only one.

"I want to thank you," she began, "from the beginning, you—"

"Don't thank me," he said.

"But—"

"I had an ulterior motive," he admitted.

"What was that?"

"Early on, I started liking your company."

She blushed; she could feel the heat reach her cheeks,

but it felt right, it felt wonderful. It was the blush of some-one who felt alive.

"Oh, that reminds me!"

"What reminds you?"

She wasn't about to tell him that his making her feel alive reminded her of something she wanted to do for him—to let him know all he'd done for her. So, instead she pulled out a business card. "This is Nate's. Seems he really enjoyed being a lone wolf. He's going to take on some cases on his own. I thought about you."

"Me, I don't have anything to hide."

"No, but you have someone to find."

The look in his eyes almost did her in. There had to be a rule or something about feeling *too* emotional, *too* in love.

"Mary. He'll find Mary. And maybe Kenny." Eric didn't say anything else. Tonight they were celebrating so much: closures, new beginnings and hope.

Then he surprised her.

"Here," he said, "I brought you something."

She took it. He hadn't wrapped it or maybe he had tried, guy-style. It was in a brown paper bag. It didn't take but a second to open.

A used Bible.

"You lost yours," he said, "in the wash."

"And you're giving me yours?"

"No, I'm giving you my mother's. She spent years teaching me about the Father. She'd be pleased to know that now I have someone else wanting to do the same."

There were fifty people in the house.

Two of them were leaning toward each other about to share both a first kiss and the beginning of a lifetime.

Dear Reader,

When I wrote *Pursuit of Justice,* Eric Santellis played such a vital role but occupied a "behind the scenes" position. He gave up more than two years of his life for his best friend, and it always bothered me that I left him in jail for a crime he didn't commit. Usually, when I finish one book and get ready to start another, story ideas tap me on the shoulder and say, "My turn." "No, me next!" "Hey, I've been waiting for five years!" There might very well be ten ideas dancing around me all demanding their turn. This time, that didn't happen. This time only one story idea stood and tapped me on the shoulder. Its name: Eric Santellis.

A strong hero deserves a strong heroine. Ruth Atkins fit the bill. You have to admire a woman who becomes a policewoman just to make sure justice is done. And, that she blamed Eric's brothers for her husband's death sure made for some interesting conflict.

The Price of Redemption is both Eric's and Ruth's stories. They are characters who know about carrying burdens. Eric's burden is his name, his family, their reputation. Ruth's burden is the inability of letting go, of forgiving, of letting compassion have a part of her life. Figuring out how God might deal with two such characters put my fingers to the keyboard.

And thanks to my readers. I hope you get to know Ruth and Eric like I did. They're survivors.

Pamela Tracy

QUESTIONS FOR DISCUSSION

1. Eric didn't hesitate to call the police when he stumbled across the first body. He knew his last name would put him under heavy scrutiny, he knew a media circus would follow, yet he did what was right. Can you think of a time you did what was right even though you knew you'd pay a price?

2. Ruth chose a dangerous profession. She did so for two main reasons: money and to keep Dustin's case open. What do you think of her choice? Her reasons? What other options might she have pursued?

3. Ruth's childhood helped shape her adulthood. What strengths did she possess because of her rough beginning? What weaknesses?

4. Did Ruth really, by the end of the book, learn compassion? Do you think she truly "owns" compassion now or will learning compassion be a lifelong endeavor?

5. Carolyn George, Ruth's mother, kept her part in Dustin's death a secret because she didn't want to put Ruth and Megan in the same danger. What would you have done?

6. When Rosa faced suspicion, some members of the community, even the church, distanced themselves. Can you think of a time when a brother or sister in

Christ stood accused of sin, and you also judged them? How did you feel? How did they react?

7. Eric intended to use his time at the cabin to recoup. He wanted to be a hermit. Yet, he never had the chance to utilize the solitude he so wanted. Based on what you know of Eric, did he really need solitude or was being involved more suited to his personality?

8. No matter the sins of the father, Eric takes care of Yano Santellis during his old age. Why?

9. Rich Mallery resigns as sheriff. He really was a "good" sheriff, except when it came to turning a blind eye to his brother. What should Rich do now? Should he also face criminal charges?

10. At the end of the book, Elizabeth Winters lies in the hospital, probably dying of pneumonia. What compassion should Ruth show Elizabeth? How do you think Elizabeth's children will react to the deeds of their parents?

INTRODUCING

Love Inspired.

HISTORICAL

A NEW TWO-BOOK SERIES.

Every month, acclaimed
inspirational authors
will bring you engaging stories
rich with romance, adventure
and faith set in a variety
of vivid historical times.

History begins on **February 12**
wherever you buy books.

Steeple
Hill®

www.SteepleHill.com

REQUEST YOUR FREE BOOKS!
2 FREE RIVETING INSPIRATIONAL NOVELS PLUS 2 FREE MYSTERY GIFTS

YES! Please send me 2 FREE Love Inspired® Suspense novels and my 2 FREE mystery gifts. After receiving them, if I don't wish to receive any more books, I can return the shipping statement marked "cancel." If I don't cancel, I will receive 4 brand-new novels every month and be billed just $3.99 per book in the U.S. or $4.74 per book in Canada, plus 25¢ shipping and handling per book and applicable taxes, if any*. That's a savings of 20% off the cover price! I understand that accepting the 2 free books and gifts places me under no obligation to buy anything. I can always return a shipment and cancel at any time. Even if I never buy another book from Steeple Hill, the two free books and gifts are mine to keep forever.

123 IDN EL5H   323 IDN ELQH

Name	(PLEASE PRINT)
Address	Apt. #
City	State/Prov. Zip/Postal Code

Signature (if under 18, a parent or guardian must sign)

Order online at www.LoveInspiredSuspense.com

Or mail to Steeple Hill Reader Service™:

IN U.S.A.: P.O. Box 1867, Buffalo, NY 14240-1867
IN CANADA: P.O. Box 609, Fort Erie, Ontario L2A 5X3

Not valid to current Love Inspired Suspense subscribers.

**Want to try two free books from another series?
Call 1-800-873-8635 or visit www.morefreebooks.com**

* Terms and prices subject to change without notice. NY residents add applicable sales tax. Canadian residents will be charged applicable provincial taxes and GST. This offer is limited to one order per household. All orders subject to approval. Credit or debit balances in a customer's account(s) may be offset by any other outstanding balance owed by or to the customer. Please allow 4 to 6 weeks for delivery.

Your Privacy: Steeple Hill is committed to protecting your privacy. Our Privacy Policy is available online at www.eHarlequin.com or upon request from the Reader Service. From time to time we make our lists of customers available to reputable firms who may have a product or service of interest to you. If you would prefer we not share your name and address, please check here. ☐

LISUS07

Love Inspired SUSPENSE

TITLES AVAILABLE NEXT MONTH

Don't miss these four stories in December

HER CHRISTMAS PROTECTOR by Terri Reed

Running from her abusive ex-husband, Faith Delange found shelter in Sisters, Oregon. But how secure was her haven? The longer she stayed, the more she endangered her new friends, including protective rancher Luke Campbell.

BURIED SINS by Marta Perry
The Three Sisters Inn

Caroline Hampton feared her husband was involved in something shady, but he died before she could confront him...didn't he? A string of dangerous incidents implied otherwise. Caroline fled to her sisters' inn, but trouble—and the suspicions of Police Chief Zachary Burkhalter—followed her home....

HARD EVIDENCE by Roxanne Rustand
Snow Canyon Ranch

Human remains were found behind the isolated cabins Janna McAllister was fixing up on her family ranch. And she suspected someone lurked out there even still. Her unexpected lodger, Deputy Sheriff Michael Robertson, made the single mother feel safe. Until she unwittingly tempted a killer out of the woodwork.

BLUEGRASS PERIL by Virginia Smith

When her boss was murdered, the police suspected single mom Becky Dennison. To clear her name, Becky teamed up with Scott Lewis, from a neighboring breeder's farm, to find the truth. In this Kentucky race, the stakes were life or death.

LISCNM1107